BEGINNING...

It was a cold, brisk evening, dusk had cascaded over the land creating shadows and secrets beyond the imagination of even the least faint of heart, in fact, it appeared darker than usual for that particular time of night. He had been watching the building for a few hours, his eyes growing tired but his focus on his mission at hand keeping them wide, waiting for those 'things' to arrive. They had been using the school as a kind of feeding ground whilst it was out for the summer. He knew they were there, there were many signs, ones that the average being would not have spotted or realised that anything was out of the ordinary; the strange prints, like feet but oddly angled, the average person would not deem them different but he knew the subtle change, then there were the patches of dead grass where their acidic dribble had fallen as they walked along, the odd, slightly pronged scratch marks that could be found along the benches and posts, and lastly, that subtle smell of death in the air that always lingered when they were around. These things, these creatures, had been plaguing the earth for as long as man, but they had all been run underground centuries ago, they were scum that fed on the humans, and they were back out in the open, and he had to find out why.

Peering around the corner he spotted one, human in appearance, very tall, long nailed, skulking along like a lion searching for prey, it had very sharp features, short dark hair, but a very pale pointy face, seeing one from a distance it could almost be human, he knew other wise. Tiptoeing toward the creature the man lifted his blade, but he was had. The vampidna quick as a flash turned to greet his assailant with a swipe of his long fingernails, more like talons Vinnie thought. He dodged to the right and jabbed with his left, but the creature evaded by ducking and swerving, again he clawed at Vinnie, this time knocking the blade from his grasp. It dropped to the ground with a clink. Vinnie jumped back narrowly avoiding being eviscerated and went in with a right hook, then a left hook, catching the vampidna by surprise it stumbled back giving Vinnie enough time to seize the blade and jab it in the creature's chest. It laughed at him.

"I can't die this way." It said. Vinnie grinned. He pulled the blade back out. The Creature clutched at his chest, a searing pain rattled through his bones.

"But I can poison you with cat's blood." Vinnie watched as it gasped and moaned before collapsing on a nearby bench. "Now I want to ask you a few questions before I end you."

"And why would I help you?" It snarled through gritted teeth.

"Why not?" Vinnie chuckled. "All I want to know is, why are you coming out of where ever it is you've been hiding, I know not all of you stay hidden but there seems to be an increase in all of the scum of the earth reappearing, I've already chased down a group of wolvenbeasts and they wouldn't talk?" The Vampidna spat out a glob of his acidic spit onto the floor.

"I have nothing to say to you, except, the king of beasts is rising." He laughed.

"The king of beasts, you mean the one who supposedly created all you weirdos, the one that could bring on an apocalypse?"

"The very same."

"When, where?"

"We all got the same message, we're to start putting the humans in their place and when he comes, well, end of the world, end of the reign of man and his weakness." His smile was bloody, but somewhat pitiful.

"That didn't answer my question, I'm sure there's a miscommunication somewhere, this beast isn't coming back." Vinnie sighed.

"You, y-you k-know nothing, you c-can't stop it," He coughed and choked as the poison started getting to him. "You don't have the h-help you once h-had."

"You'd be surprised." Vinnie watched as the pathetic inhuman wretched and spluttered until it took its last breath. He thought for a moment, if what that ugly critter said was true, then the world was about to get a whole lot crazier.

1.

Many moons ago, when all creatures walked the earth, a special group of, mostly, humans, known collectively as the Oringorgons, were in a great battle with the millions of monsters that were trying to rule the world. They consisted of Vampidna's – a vampire like creature, with the ability to suck a humans flesh down to the bone with their acidic spit and fangs, they were deadly afraid of cats, and a cats blood was poison to them, Wolvenbeasts – Part wolf, part bear, part human, the ability to transform from human to wolf with the size and power of a brown bear, a blade to the heart does the trick with those ones, Hexhers and Hexhims – basically witches and wizards but they could only use old school spells and hexes, killing them was much the challenge but trapping them with their own spell would usually help, that or voodoo, there were other things too, like werecats, shifters, ghosts, enchanted ones, smoke people, elementals and more, but they were very hit and miss whose side they were on, some worked with the humans and some against, friendships were never completely set in stone when it came to the battle of power. When the ultimate battle took place, the king of beasts, a tall skeletal man with boned wings which were shredded and torn, a skull for a face with ripped flesh all around, holes where his eyes should be, and always wearing a top hat, tried to take over the world, but he failed. One man and his friends fought long and hard until they discovered how to send the beast into an oblivion – a cage essentially, that could only be opened with 3 very specific keys that were well hidden, or so the story was told, no one really knew how the beast was kept locked away. The earth was saved, many savage monsters were run into hiding or killed, the odd few cropping up now and again and hunted by remaining Oringorgons and everything continued as if it had never happened, the oblivious humans unaware of the real monsters that were out there.

Reading the story of his great, great, great, great and so on, grandfather, Vinnie let out a huge sigh.

"How, how can the king of beasts be rising what do they mean by rising, he was locked in a cage of some sort for centuries right, doesn't he die, where are the keys?"

"No, he doesn't die or he'd have been killed all those years ago as a preventative right, not locked in a cage," Cooper shrugged. "I have no idea where the keys are or what the keys are, but someone must know, if all the bad guys received the same message, someone will be able to tell us, not everyone, or everything can be that loyal."

"Peachy."

"I think it's more likely that a key or whatever is needed for his release, has been found, maybe two, or else they wouldn't be so confident, the fact he is rising and not yet risen says to me they're still not quite there yet, they're looking for the last of something." Lydia sipped at her cup of hot chocolate, she was always drinking hot chocolate, Vinnie thought, and she had an endless supply. There were nods in agreement between the three friends.

Vinnie, Cooper and Lydia had been friends for a long time, years in fact, they met at school and after some odd happenings, discoveries and saving each other's lives, they remained best friends all these years later – the occasional monster or evil spirit would crop up and they would dispose of them together, they had quite the little business going in that respect, people, or those that were aware of the 'supernatural' aspect to life, would often call for an exorcism or discarding of some kind of beast in their back garden for instance, and the three monster-tiers would rock up and fight them off, the only problem being all three believing their plan was right or their plan should go ahead first, friendships are difficult when you are all great leaders.

"So, what are we going to do about it, I mean, we can't let this happen, it would be catastrophic to, to, well, I guess the whole of mankind?" Cooper flicked through a book that once belonged to Vinnie's father, it held many a tale about beasts and how to kill or trap them.

"I say we look for a key, if it exists," Lydia said. "Even if they have two, we get the third, beast can't get out without all three right, he is not getting let out of his cage, as long as he remains there, world isn't in imminent danger?"

"Stupid idea, for starters it's not been confirmed that there are physical keys, it was a story that there were three keys to lock the cage yet nobody has ever seen them, and even if there are, where the hell do we start, if nobody's seen them, nobody knows if they even exist, we'll be looking for a needle in a hay stack, one tiny needle in one multi-storey, heavily guarded, probably on fire haystack?!" Cooper sniffed.

"Actually, it's not a bad idea, someone has obviously found something relating to those potential keys or they wouldn't be coming out of the woodwork saying the beast is coming back, so we have to find that someone that knows, or has some knowledge of what we could be looking for." Vinnie sighed. As he stood up, he pulled out his phone from his pocket. Skimming through his contacts list of numbers he found one that he hovered over for a moment, it was the number of a woman called Intention, thinking out loud he said. "Let's hope she's in a charitable mood, I'm in no disposition to be cursed." He listened to the tone and the blatant chill in the voice that answered with his name. "Intention," He cleared his throat still thinking why the hell anyone would name their kid that. "I was calling - "

"About the keys to the cage of the beastly king, yes, I know, I'm a Gyporer, I see all remember?" He could hear the sheer patronising tone in her voice, as per usual. "I can of course look into where you may find one, because I know that's what you want, but you have to do something for me first."

"I didn't doubt that in - "

"Of course, it won't be easy."

"It never is, what – "

"I need the venom of a Serpenmamba, dangerous, vile things, but their venom is useful to me you see, if you can collect some and bring it to me, I will locate a key for you." Intention let out a big sigh.

"A Serpenmamba, of course," Vinnie gritted his teeth. "No problem, and where can I find one, I thought they were extinct?"

"Not far from where you are my dear, in actual fact Vinnie there is just one left alive," She laughed. "And I believe it may be stalking you." The line went dead. Vinnie put his phone in his pocket and retrieved his blade from the table, it was an odd looking thing, slightly curved with one side made of silver the other made of iron, along the handle carved delicately was the word 'Protego' meaning 'I protect or I defend' and that exact blade had been in Vinnie's family for as long as he could remember, passed down through the generations of Oringorgons.

"What's happening?" Cooper questioned.

"Serpenmamba, Intention said there's one following us, she needs its venom." Vinnie whispered. Cooper screwed up his nose. Serpenmamba were human in form but covered in scales, with the forked tongue of a snake and the deadly poison of a black mamba, they were nasty creatures that would stalk and feed on its unsuspecting prey, first poisoning it with just enough to cause excruciating pain before eating their victim whilst they were still alive, not the nicest death. Lydia stood up, and from out of her bag she pulled a small container, a vial. Both she and Vinnie had enchanted items that allowed them to carry more than normal, Lydia her bag and Vinnie his jacket. She waved the vial at them.

"Okay," She said. "You hold it down whilst I take the venom."

"Shouldn't we just kill it, be easier to extract without the potential of, well, you know, dying?" Cooper asked. Lydia smiled.

"Ah, my naïve little Cooperim, their venom is only extractable whilst they are a living form, the moment they die it dries up."

"Brilliant," Vinnie said sarcastically. "Let's do this then I suppose."

2.

They were in a cabin in the woods, a convenient place to kill for a stalking monster, it was the place they fixed up together a few years back as a 'safe space' to hide out when necessary, meet each other were they to ever split up on missions – which was a very rare occurrence, and to plan things, anything from a holiday to the next monster hunt. Vinnie gently pulled back a curtain with his blade, and peered out of the grotty window, it was dark outside and very still, almost too quiet for such an area that would normally be thriving with creatures of the night, like owls, it was as if all nature's mortals and monsters for that matter had disappeared, hidden or simply run away. He nodded at the other two and exited the cabin through the creaky wooden door, cringing as the squeak rang out into the silent night. He immediately felt a chill, the hairs on the back of his neck stood up, he could sense something watching him. Acting entirely normal, as to not arouse suspicion, he kept his hand clutched tightly around his blade in his jacket pocket, and walked toward his car, once there he opened the boot, pretending to look for something, pretending not to hear his assailant. Something was coming alright, he listened intently, honing in on the thing he sensed, he could hear the heavy breathing of a monster on the prowl, he could feel it getting closer, when the twig snapped just feet behind him, he spun around and quick as a flash, punched the ugly bastard in the middle of his face. It groaned and recoiled before baring its manky yellow teeth, and again, this time with more purpose it lunged toward Vinnie. He went to pull the knife from his pocket in a swift act of heroism, but unfortunately, and not unlike Vinnie, it got stuck, so to avoid being Serpenmamba chow he used his bare hands to grapple the dreadful thing. Wrestling the disgusting beast who snarled and scratched at him, Vinnie managed to hook his arm around its neck and drag it toward the cabin. Cooper and Lydia came bounding out, Lydia chanting in her native tongue that sounded much like gobbledygook to Vinnie's ear, Cooper pulled open the Serpenmamba's mouth, carefully avoiding getting bitten and dying in an agonising, untimely fashion, as Vinnie fought to keep the sneering creature still, Lydia placed her small container on the biggest tooth in the monsters mouth and continued to chant, she watched as the vial began to fill with a thick yellowy gloop, when it was full she stopped and put the lid on. Cooper fished the blade from Vinnie's pocket and stabbed it into the fiend's skull. It screeched in pain and as Vinnie let go its body dissolved in front of their eyes. Lydia held up the ampule of gross gloop with a smile.

"That was easy."

"Yeah for you two, I'm the one that nearly gets killed in these cases." Vinnie said. Lydia rolled her eyes. "Let's take this crap to intentionally irritating and find out where one of these keys are."

They had been driving for around two hours when Vinnie pulled over to a petrol station.

"I'm hungry, and I need coffee." He said. The other two nodded in agreement, the dreary looks upon their faces the personification of fatigue, and the three of them got out of the vehicle, then they entered the store, Vinnie had used it regularly on his travels and knew that it had a little café inside which did some great coffee. After buying their beverages and extra slices of cake at the counter, they sat down at a table. All was quiet as they munched on their sweet treats. Lydia scanned the café.

"Is it just me, or is it a little bit too quiet in here, not unlike outside the cabin, don't you think?" She asked. Vinnie and Cooper looked around too, their eyes passing over the contents of the area. There were a few people present, not many, but they were still, totally unmoving, as if frozen in time, there were two sat at a table together, one on her own and another, an employee of the store, Standing with a mop, not physically cleaning, but staring at the thing like it was talking to him.

"Somethings not right." Cooper agreed. As if they had just done something outrageously offensive or crazy, all four people present turned to face the three friends. "Definitely not right." Cooper gulped. Suddenly, the fours skin began to turn a deep shade of purple, their eyes a dark glowing green and their hair started to fall out until they were left with a bald head full of lumpy bumps. Like magic, they also grew a few feet taller, with needle like nails, jagged teeth, and some mangled, oddly angled feet. Vinnie, Cooper and Lydia had gotten to a Standing position by this point, each retrieving their own choice of weapon from their pockets, Vinnie's was his blade, the family heirloom that he would never be without, Lydia's an incredibly sharp, magical, pointy crystal and Cooper, well Cooper was his own weapon, he was a shifter, a shapeshifter, a good one at that, he could shift into any creature desired, well normal shifters of his stature could, Cooper had only been able to shift into a Siberian Husky for all of his life, he did not know why, it was the only thing he had ever been able to manage, anything else failed, or he would revert to the Husky, but the Husky was indeed a powerful tool. The brutes grinned at them.

"Ah, the three pursuers, you have a reputation for causing the monster world problems." One of the fiends said with a lisp. He and the other three created a kind of semi-circle a short distance from the friends.

"And we're about to cause you some, you ugly son of a bitch." Vinnie replied. They were damn ugly, they were called Dragums; derivatives of a kind of human, dragon hybrid, they were once much more elegant, beautiful creatures, their purple skin was smooth and bright, their green eyes shimmered, they had amazing mains of hair in varying colours, the majority had also had large, scaled wings, but as the years passed it was certainly not kind to them, they were tortured and slaughtered and bred in captivity, causing defects and abnormalities and became things so grotesque they were shunned by all, shunned simply because they were not what they used to be, because for the many of that era, beauty was more important than anything else. They became extremely angry and resentful from then on and a bunch of murdering bastards, that of course, Vinnie and the gang were in charge of putting down. Charging each other, the three friends clashed with the Dragums, their needle nails were extremely strident and tough and as Vinnie struck strikes with his blade one of them countered with a swipe and the clink of metal rang through their eardrums, Vinnie went in for another jab and the ugly beast grabbed his arms, as they tussled, Lydia chanted at her sharp crystal causing it to glow blue, she then swished at the legs of one of the creatures who fell in pain as it sliced through the solid bone-like flesh, and as it fell to its knees, she then sliced it across the throat and it collapsed fully to the floor, she then stabbed it in the back of the neck, causing it to shriek. When she pulled the crystal out, the body disappeared in a puff of purple smoke, leaving behind a purple sooty residue. Meanwhile Cooper, as Husky dog, bit and tore at another Dragum, His teeth clamping down on its arm, very dark, almost black blood seeped out, the monster tried to claw at him and he let go, quickly diving through the beasts legs and turning around to bite it in the ass, it screamed and fell over, Cooper let go and jumped on the monsters head using his teeth to bite its neck clean off of its body with his mighty jaws, it too disappeared in a puff of smoke. Vinnie had managed to escape his tussle and jammed his knife through the heart of the Dragum, killing it instantly, another attacked him but this time he pulled out his gun and shot it in the head, and he lowered the gun and waited for the smoke to evaporate. The three friends sighed.

"All I wanted was a nice drink and a little bit to eat, is that too much to ask?" Vinnie Sighed.

"It's normal for us, you know that, I'm also inclined to think that we're going to be on the monsters most wanted list for trying to stop their King rising, he's like their messiah isn't he, it's unlikely we'll ever get a nice meal?" Lydia replied with a sad face. As they picked up their coffees to go, they began to walk out.

"Wait," Came a shrill cry from the counter. "What the fuck just happened?" It was the guy who had served them, he was still human, and the three had totally forgotten about him. Lydia walked over to him and pulled out a little vial of clear liquid from her backpack.

"Drink," She said, a little sparkle in her eye. "You need it." He took it from her and without question, he drank it. He fell in a heap to the floor. "He'll think it was all a dream when he wakes up." They exited the café and got back into the vehicle.

"How much longer to intentions place?" Cooper asked as he wiped blood from his now human face with his torn t-shirt, Lydia had managed to enchant Cooper's clothes to remain on his human form when he transformed, but she had not quite perfected the state they came back in.

"About four or five hours, I told you it was a long drive, you need to get your portal making game on Lyds," Vinnie said, she rolled her eyes, it was something she had not yet managed to master. "We'll stop at a hotel in about an hour, do the last three or so in the morning, it'll be easier to spot the bad guys in the day, my eyes sometimes deceive me, and I'm getting too old for this shit." They all laughed as he pulled the vehicle back onto the road once more.

3.

They each got separate rooms in the hotel, said their goodnights and went to bed. Vinnie lay awake for a while, thinking about the task at hand, could they really stop a gazillion freakishly determined freaks from bringing back their beloved god, the one thing that could potentially end all of humanity with barely a click of its fingers? He did not know, but they were going to try of course, it was one hell of a weight to hold on the shoulders of the three of them though. He listened to the sounds of the outside, passing cars, a light breeze, the annoying yappy dog in another room somewhere, who allows pets in a hotel anyway? Then he thought, Cooper is kind of a pet, he chuckled to himself and gradually drifted off into a dreamy sleep or a nightmarish one, time would tell.

The woman of his dreams disappeared as he was awoke with a start. He could hear banging at his door, loud and insistent, he sensed urgency. Jumping out of bed, wobbling a little with his groggy head, he pulled up his trousers and chucked a t-shirt on. Picking up his gun from the little table at the edge of the room, he decided instantly he was not in the mood for a knife fight, he creeped toward the thumping door. Lifting the gun to shoulder height he gently opened the door a crack. Cooper was stood on the other side looking shocked to see a weapon in his face. Vinnie lowered the gun and opened the door wide, walked away and Cooper walked in and shut the door behind him. Vinnie put the gun back on the table and lent against it.

"Were you going to shoot me?" Cooper asked, the shock obvious in his voice.

"No, what's with the rude awakening?"

"Seriously, you heard me, and you were going to shoot, if you weren't going to shoot why the gun, huh?"

"I didn't shoot you, why are you banging on my door at half six in the morning Cooper, we've only been trying to sleep for a few hours?!" Vinnie looked at the clock on his phone and threw it down on the table angrily, he was an angry man on little sleep, and sleep deprivation was a sure-fire way of causing an impossibly grouchy, argumentative Vinnie.

"I'm sorry, but a gun, really?" Cooper said and judging by the look on Vinnie's face he realised he was not going to get an apology for the gun in the face. "Okay, fine, forget about the gun – "

"Cooper, just tell me why the sudden urgency before I change my mind and really do shoot you."

"Well," Cooper cleared his throat. Vinnie rolled his eyes, that usually meant Cooper was about to go into never-ending bullshit story mode. "Basically, Lydia knocked on my door about twenty minutes ago, or maybe thirty, yeah, yeah I'd say it was more like thirty minutes ago, she said couldn't sleep, she was on edge, she was pacing, you know how she does, and she sensed something, something unnatural, then she said she heard crying babies, then children and women and men and more babies, and then she asked could I hear anything, I said no I couldn't and I have good hearing, you know, being part of a dog and all, and she said she was going to have a look, suss the place, check it out, she is of the belief that there may be spirits or ghosts, ghostly apparitions, whatever you want to call them, here, and quite possibly not the happy kind, maybe not on poltergeist level, but possibly a little um, vengeful, and I said let's wake you up, and she said no she won't be gone long, you know what he's like on zero sleep, I said I know he's a dick and she left and I followed her for about fifteen minutes or so, maybe, maybe it was ten, twenty – "

"Cooper, I don't need your life story, where is Lydia, what else did she say about these ghosts, need I remind the both of you we haven't got time for this shit?" Vinnie interrupted. Cooper walked over to the table and helped himself to Vinnie's stash of sweets he had just spotted.

"Well," He said chewing noisily. "She said they are probably malevolent, and there's probably more than one, and they may even have the ability to possess humans – "

"Okay, so we're dealing with asshole ghosts, probably been stuck here a long time and its making them pissy, so has Lydia found any, or is she on a wild goose chase, because honestly, stopping a real evil dude from rising to earth and potentially causing the end of humanity seems a little more important than helping a little town rid a couple of ghosts, or am I missing the point?"

"That's the thing, she said she could hear a baby, in distress, you know what people are like with babies in distress, they feel all, maternal and want to help, she walked into the woods and then poof, she was gone, then I came here." Cooper swallowed the sweet he had been annoyingly chewing for the whole conversation. Vinnie raised an eyebrow.

"So, you lost her, we have a missing Lydia, some potentially angry spirits and maybe even some possessions, excellent," He sighed. "Suppose we better get to it then, because I ain't getting back to sleep now."

"Oh, and there is one other thing, that may or may not, likely may, make you very angry," Cooper grimaced. "The car has also um, how do I put this, just uh, gone, disappeared, vanished, not sure if it's ghosts related, or just plain theft." Vinnie rolled his eyes; he could feel the heat boiling in his cheeks from the pure anger he was trying to regress.

"Just peachy." He said through gritted teeth.

They gathered their belongings, which was mostly bits and bobs in backpacks consisting of weaponry, clothing, wash products stolen from hotels, and snacks, what with being on the road for most of their lives they had no need for huge amounts of possessions most of which also fitted into the enchanted pockets on Vinnie's jacket giving him the ability to carry lots without the weight, they call it his 'jacket of tricks', and then they headed into the little town.

"Where do we start?" Cooper asked. Vinnie pointed toward a coffee shop, Cooper nodded, his thought process being that if Vinnie at least got his coffee he would be somewhat bearable, and in they went. Ordering two coffees Vinnie struck up a conversation with the barista.

"So, this town is nice, people are friendly, quite close knit, I bet you all know each other by first name, don't you?" He asked. The young lady laughed.

"Yeah most of us do, the people here are lovely, it's just a little um," She paused. "Creepy, don't get me wrong it's cute, quaint, but it's just a little creepy."

"Creepy, I suppose it is a little isn't it, let me guess; there's a tale in this town and it's all about a premises or a graveyard or a certain area around here that's haunted?" Vinnie took his coffee as the young woman whose name tag said 'Lucy' handed it to him and he proceeded to add copious amounts of sugar to it.

"You're spot on there, although not just ghosts." She smiled.

"Not just ghosts, what else could there be then, in these tales?" He said not only pretending to be intrigued anymore but showing real interest as he wondered what other frightening creatures he has to face.

"Babies." She replied. Vinnie raised an eyebrow, not in a condescending way, more of an 'okay I may be alright after all' kind of look.

"Babies," He said mockingly. "Last I heard they were living, breathing little poop units, nothing creepy about them, well, except maybe the amount of poop they produce, that's a little scary – "

"Not baby-babies, not the cute little crawling balls of snot, no, these babies are different, legend has it that this town used to be home to these weird gargoyle type creatures, they were like vampires but much older, uglier, weird greying skin and pointy faces, not the type you see in the movies these days anyway, and they reproduced as males and females do, but man came along and took a dislike to these things so hunted and killed all the parents, because the parents would leave the nests to find food so were easy to catch, but the babies were well hidden, so when the parents died the babies were left to fend for themselves, they escaped or survived whatever way you want to look at it, and made their home in the deepest darkest part of the woods, apparently, if you go into the woods alone and you hear a baby crying in distress, you must run in the opposite direction, because that's exactly how they lure you in, they cry to show vulnerability, they look so sweet and innocent that you think they're defenceless, but once you let down your guard and show them some interest, or pick them up they'll turn and eat you, some say they remain looking like babies just grow teeth and fangs, others say they become full on monsters, everyone who claims to have seen them have their version, either way, they aren't to be messed with, oh and the ghost part of the story is simply that there were many people, mainly women, that didn't come back out of those woods once entering, apparently they heard the cries of babes and the motherly instinct kicked in, unfortunately that's what those things prey on, and a few men have been lost looking for their wives, so people believed they'd been eaten and their spirits haunt the woods too, although some spirits have allegedly made their way into the town to haunt us all, well, that's what crazy old lady Marge says up the road." She explained. Vinnie nodded.

"Right, double whammy, baby monsters, ghosts, add the crazy old ladies and we have ourselves a freak show," He smiled at Lucy who smiled back, he then picked up Cooper's coffee. "Thank you, pleasure talking to you." He joined Cooper at a table.

"So, what are we dealing with?" Cooper asked sipping at his drink.

"She had to go in the bloody woods didn't she?"

4.

They were stood just on the outskirts of the woods, beside one of the many trails that flowed through the trees only to be swallowed up by the darkness, Vinnie had his gun in his coat pocket and his blade in his hand, he contemplated their next move, this was a vast woodland, Lydia could be anywhere, or she could be monster meat. Cooper stared into the gloomy mass of huge trees wondering if their friend was okay, he did not think they would flourish without her, Vinnie was his best friend but they often clashed and although they were both good fighters, they did not always use the most intelligent route, Lydia was a strategist whereas Vinnie and Himself were shoot first ask questions later kind of guys.

"I think we should stick together." Cooper broke the stern silence. Vinnie agreed to Cooper's surprise.

"Yeah, let's get this over with shall we." He began walking along the trail into the shadowy and despondent woods, Cooper close behind.

It was not long before they heard strange noises, neither could decide if they were real or just their minds playing tricks on them, either way they had yet to come across anything remotely frightening.

"Maybe this is a labyrinth and it's not a case of people getting eaten, they just can't get back out again, so die of hunger and exhaustion."

"Thanks Cooper, very optimistic." Vinnie stopped so suddenly Cooper almost bumped straight into him. "Do you hear that?" He asked. Cooper listened and slowly nodded his head.

"I've been hearing that for a while, I thought it was my imagination."

"Definitely a crying baby." They slowly skulked toward the sound, each tip toe much noisier than they wanted or anticipated, both cringed with every accidental snap of a twig. Peering around a tree there was a small clearing and, in the middle, on a patch of grass, was a baby, Vinnie would guess the age to be somewhere around nine, ten months, it was sat in just a nappy, whining and rubbing its teary eyes, completely non-threatening.

"What do we do?" Cooper whispered.

"You go and pick it up, and I'll wait here, then I'll follow you and see if it takes you to Lydia." Vinnie replied.

"Why don't you go pick it up and I'll follow?" Cooper growled. Vinnie rolled his eyes. He put his blade through his belt, gave Cooper a shove as he walked past and headed toward the innocent looking little thing. Getting closer it really appeared to be a small human baby, probably tired and hungry, wondering where its parents were. It turned to him as he was just feet away, smiled and giggled, then began to crawl away, giggling an infectious little laugh that was almost enchanting Vinnie enough to believe this was a real baby, he kept telling himself in his head it was not, but his eyes were surely deceiving him. Following it back into the woods, the baby seemed to pick up speed it did not occur to him that it was odd he found himself going into a slow jog. Suddenly, he felt a massive gust of wind, then something caused him to stop as if he had hit a brick wall, he was freezing cold, he could see his own breath, and right in front of him, was a woman, her skin was very pale, her eyes were dark and sunken in, her lips a purplish blue, her hair, like a frame around her face, was a mousy brown colour, it appeared limp and greasy and quite obviously, had specks of blood in it. She had been wearing what gave the impression to be a silver dress, but it was covered in red stains, more blood. She was a ghost it seemed, but she did not look as if she was either angry or vengeful, it was fear that he could see in those dead eyes, she pointed back to where Vinnie came from and mouthed something, he did not get it at first, but soon realised she was telling him to run, run, run. She was giving him a warning. It was too late however, the creature had spotted Vinnies otherworldly warning and had crawled to his leg, without a properly processed thought, Vinnie bent down and instinctively picked up the baby. Only, it was no longer a baby, its skin had gone from smooth and beige to grey and prickly, it's cute baby face was now twisted in anger, its ears pointy and it had grown lots of tiny fangs along with sharp claws. It bit down on Vinnies arm and he yelped in pain, Cooper came out of the shadows and cringed as he punched the baby who remained clamped in place.

"Get it off, get it off!" Vinnie shouted. Cooper tried to pull it but it was tearing away Vinnies flesh. "You're going to have to shoot it or something!" Vinnie punched at the creature, not at all feeling the guilt of punching a child in the moment, it was trying to tear him apart after all. The ghost woman seemed to watch with a smug 'I told you so' look on her face. Cooper fished for Vinnies gun from his pocket and as Vinnie held his arm up, Cooper shot it twice. It immediately let go squealing, a grey ooze coming from the newly made holes. Cooper shot it once more and it died instantly. "Fuck!" Vinnie held his bloody injured arm. "I think it, was drinking my blood, it's a fucking mini vampire." The ghost woman mouthed run, run, run again, for some reason, although irrelevant to the story, some ghosts could talk, others could not, this one was in the latter, then she disappeared as quickly as she appeared in the first place.

"Oh shit!" Cooper bellowed, as in their line of sight, like a swarm, at least fifty of these mini, blood-sucking, baby bastards were crawling, very fast, towards them. Their snarls and cries now piercing to the ears. "Run!" They turned and began to run in the opposite direction of the hoard, dodging trees, jumping over logs and ducking under branches. One jumped on Cooper's back and he shot it in the head, it fell with a thud. Another two clung onto Vinnies legs causing him to slow and almost trip, he got his blade and hacked at one who let go leaving its lacerated hands behind, he then chopped at the second, lodging the weapon in its head. Continuing to run he shook the blade until the creature flung off it. Cooper shot at the closest things before the gun began to click, indicating an end to bullets. Running as fast as they could they eventually saw the light at the end of the tunnel, reaching the part of the woods of which they entered they continued to run until they reached the car park. Turning back the creatures were gone, as if they had never been there, as if the lads had in fact been running from nothing.

"What the actual hell Vin?" Cooper panted. Vinnie shook his head.

"I think we need to pay a little old lady a visit, I just hope Lydia is hiding and has not been caught."

Crazy old Marge was a large, miserable, old bat with a disregard for manners. When invited into her home the two friends found themselves fixing things, cleaning up and making her tea. Once she had been satisfied with their services, they sat, each with a cup of tea and a biscuit, opposite her on the sofas.

"So, you want to know what the creatures in the woods are, and if your friend is alive?" She asked.

"Yes we – "

"Most people don't believe there are creatures in the woods," She lowered her glasses to the bottom of her nose. "Why do you?"

"Well, Marge, we've um, we've seen them, in the flesh," Vinnie showed her his newly bandaged injury. "One of them bit me, we shot it." Marge laughed.

"In the head I hope."

"Yes actually."

"Good, only headshots, drowning and burning seem to work with those little blighters, or so I've found, those ever to survive them have found ways of killing, or they wouldn't have survived." She laughed again.

"What are they, what is it they want, is there any way of distraction, enough to find our friend?"

"They are a variation of a Tiyanak, a baby like creature that eats you, some think they're baby vampires, others think they're gargoyles or gremlins or ghouls, it depends who you ask, they are like any other vampire, they hunt, they feed, human and animal blood, they also eat people after draining them of their blood though, I think because they are kids after all, always hungry!" She explained. "As for distraction, not really, although fire may help, it's a way of killing them so can cause them to focus on survival as opposed to eating your face, I wouldn't bet on your friend still being alive though."

"I'm optimistic that she is," Vinnie replied. "Is there anything else you can tell us that might help?"

"Yes, I'd give up the search and live to tell another tale, your friend is baby-vamp food and you will be too, now, get the fuck out of my house!" She pointed a shotgun at them and very quickly they jumped to their feet and scurried out of her house. "Good luck," She called after them. "You're going to need it."

"Daft old bint." Vinnie sighed.

"The plan," Cooper said. "Set the forest on fire?"

"Read my mind, my friend."

"Great minds and all that."

They had spent very little time collecting jerry cans and filling them with petrol. Buying a collection of lighters at a different shop, to avoid suspicion, they returned to the scene of the freaky babies.

"Wow, this is really bad for the environment." Cooper said as they began pouring the petrol over trees, logs and bushes close to the clearing in which they were almost meat before.

"Those ugly little people eaters are really bad for the world." Vinnie said, flicking the lighter which sparked the flame. He could hear angry growls now, no more crying babies, these things knew that those two were not taking the bait. They appeared in a much bigger mass this time, all grey and ugly, little fangs bared, clawing at the ground, rushing toward them. He lit a small branch and threw it on the ground as they entered the clearing. In an instant, the flames ignited with an almighty roar, spreading wildly, the heat already reaching an incredible intensity. The first row of Tiyanak cried and screamed as they were burned to ash, the next rows stopping to stare in awe and fear of the dancing flames. Making a break for it the friends ran around the flames and past the captivated Tiyanak, further into the woods in a bid to find Lydia.

It was amazing how far those woods, or rather, forest, continued to delve, ever deeper and darker, they began calling Lydia's name as it was pretty certain they were no longer in close proximity to the little gnashing beasts.

"What if they did get her Vin?" Cooper asked.

"They didn't."

"But what – "

"They didn't Cooper, it's Lydia, she's not going to go down that way, not by creepy little baby vampires, she's better than that, she'll go spectacularly, we all will." Vinnie said reassuringly. That had been their pact after all; to look after each other, to save people, to rid the world of weird beasts and entities and to die spectacularly. Cooper turned his head slightly to one side, before Vinnie could blink, Cooper was in his husky dog form, sniffing the ground and listening intently.

"I can hear her!" He barked. Setting off in a sprint he dashed onwards, Vinnie trying to keep up, Cooper stopping and sniffing occasionally until he reached two oddly shaped trees. He was suddenly thrown back, his body slamming against a tree. Vinnie tried to react, but he too was thrown by an immense force, landing beside his buddy, they slowly stood, Cooper back in human form and gasped at the sheer amount of beings surrounding them, ethereal beings, spirits, and none looked particularly happy. There were at least ten women of all ages, several men and even a couple of children. Their ghost forms were bedraggled, covered in marks, bites, scratches and bloody, victims of the Tiyanak. The friends looked at each other, a look of contempt on their faces. It happened quickly, the spirits began to attack, punching and swiping like they were still in their bodies, and unfortunately for the boys, these ghosts had mastered the whole poltergeist object moving, human beating ability. The two of them fought back however, every punch they received they threw one back only to go straight through the beings and ending up either splatting themselves on a tree or face-planting the floor.

"This is no use Vin, they're freaking ghosts, and we can't punch a freaking ghost!"

"Then we try to move them on," Vinnie grunted as he picked himself up and received a sucker punch to the jaw. Holding his hand out in front of him he said. "Tempus est ad eam movere in Melius referet, mecumque relinque mundum et vivi et abiit in spiritu orbis." Some of the spirits stopped in their tracks, lights shone from the sky and they disappeared in a heavenly glow, others, however, remained in their angry willing to kill the living state.

"Relinquo, relinquo, ad movere, spirituum et abierunt!" Cooper shouted. A livid woman, hair unkempt, arms cut to shreds let out a shrill cry before charging him and lifting him off the ground by his neck. She squeezed his throat so tightly he was struggling to breath. Vinnie could not get over to help as he had his own mad man lunging at him, he dodged several blows, frustrated that he could not land his own. It was a sudden moment when everything seemed to go eerily quiet, that the two guys realised they were no longer getting beaten, instead the spirits had stopped, dead in their tracks, Cooper was released from his death grip and he clutched at his neck gasping for air. Vinnie slinked over to him and helped him to his feet.

"Are you okay?"

"Yeah." Cooper croaked. The ghosts were in some sort of trance, it was clear they were fearful of something, they were listening, but the lads could not hear anything, it was not until the spirits began to disappear one after the other of their own accord that they realised something was coming, and as they turned to look behind them, they saw the Tiyanak pack racing toward them, like hundreds of oversized ants. That was what the ghosts were afraid of, their killers. Giving each other the 'shit we better run' look, Vinnie and Cooper ran toward the oddly shaped trees, they were odd because they bent in towards each other, as if reaching to one another ready for an embrace, or a tree-hug. As they reached the trees, they felt an immense force pulling them towards the middle of them, so much so they stopped and yet continued to be dragged toward the trees, looking between the trees and the Tiyanak, the friends were not sure what was for the best. Unable to turn back they allowed the pull of the trees to drag them and as they passed through the middle they saw a bright blue light and were suddenly not in the woods anymore.

5.

It was, or what appeared to be, a small village. Not an ordinary village you might come across today, but on old school one, with mediocre houses that had straw rooves and wooden walls, they looked like shacks. One of the doors opened, and from out of one of the houses came a woman with beautiful tan skin and long, curly brunette hair, a small smile on her lips, it was Lydia.

"Cooper, Vinnie!" She exclaimed, running over she embraced them both. "You heard me?"

"I did, but I didn't know to walk through the bloody trees, that was fun!" Cooper replied. Lydia laughed.

"I didn't either, after running from those monster babies I felt this strange force pulling me towards the trees, as if it was coming from the trees themselves, I went through the middle and ended up here, it's such a beautiful place."

"Where exactly is here, where are we?" Vinnie questioned. Looking around it seemed strangely unoccupied, as if those that had once belonged had left in a hurry. As lovely as it appeared, it had an aura of uncertainty, eeriness plagued the very air they were breathing.

"It's another realm, an actual other realm, which are never easy to find let me tell you, it's called Crypskie, and luckily, those horrible little bloody things can't pass through the portal, thank goodness, they turn to dust if they try so have learnt to steer clear."

"Another realm, wow," Cooper smiled. "What's here, are there weird creatures, mythical ones, something really magical?"

"Or something really deadly?" Vinnie added. Lydia sighed.

"Both actually, and the good guys really need our help, and I think we should."

"Help them, Lyds, who are the good guys, and what exactly are we up against, because honestly at this rate we are never going to find out where that damn key is and by the time we get back home we'll probably find the apocalypse has happened or something just as drastic?" Vinnie was so matter of fact; Lydia sometimes wondered if he ever had good thoughts.

"You can meet the good ones, and the good thing about here is, time is not as fast, you see, a day in Crypskie is like an hour in our world, so we won't miss too much, there's a secret hideout through the houses, it's like doctor who's Tardis it's amazing, where they're all holed up at the moment, as for the bad guys, eh," She shrugged. "There are the usual vampires, werewolves and the odd Tauranion, not too bad, but, unfortunately, there are also Gashadokuros and Dover demons." Vinnie groaned.

"Peachy."

"Oh, come on, we have to help them Vin, there are Elveens, fairies, centaurs, pixies and mermaids here, they need us, the majority are such peaceful creatures that don't know how to fight, at least if we teach them, they'll be better defended, they can defend themselves, even if we don't stay for it all, we can give them an advantage." She explained.

"Elveens, centaurs, mermaids, aw come on Vin, please let's help, please?" Cooper grinned. Vinnie frowned.

"Well we're here now I suppose."

"Yay." Cooper and Lydia said in unison.

"Come on, come and meet the good guys."

It was not every day you got to meet a mythical creature, there were rumours on the grapevine when Vinnie was young that the stories were true, and the existence of fairies, unicorns and what-not else were true, but many thought it to be made up nonsense, despite the fight against such creatures as vampires and werewolves, so why could the likes of centaurs not be true too? Lydia took them through one of the houses, it really was like the Tardis, tiny on the outside, huge on the inside, it had multiple rooms and multiple corridors, leading them down one of the right-hand corridors, Lydia stopped still at a wall.

"Aperta sesame." She waved her hand over the wall and like magic the bricks began to pop and bang until they disappeared leaving another hallway in view. Walking down it, which seemed to go on forever, the walls a mixture of blurred colours, they reached a big, bold green door. Lydia knocked seven times, a few quiet and a few louder with her knuckles and waited. They could hear all the different locks and chains undoing before the heavy door swung open of its own accord. Inside was what could only be described as a rose-golden room, brightly lit and full of beautiful tapestries, paintings and a huge rose-gold table. Sat at the table was a spectacular bunch of beasts. The trio stepped inside and the door closed by itself behind them.

There were two Elveens sat at the table, a male and female, they were like a cross between an elf and a supermodel, such striking beautiful creatures, their hair white with black streaks, their ears pointy, tall, slender figures and they wearing white and gold suits, casual suits, like flowing trousers and loose jackets, white with pin striped gold. There was also a few bright and colourful fairies, pixies and dwarves in what appeared to be work wear, and there was a centaur, half man half horse, incredibly muscular and fierce looking, like a warrior. There was also an avian humanoid, a man with wings - he too looked strong and fierce, his grey wings were folded in at his back, but he remained stood at the table.

"Lydia, is this the friends you've been talking about?" Said the winged man.

"Yes, this is Vinnie and Cooper," She said pointing at them.

"Cooper, Vinnie, this is Kalmin." She introduced them to birdman who strolled over to them, his magnificent wings flowing behind him, and shook their hands one by one.

"Nice to meet you Vinnie and Cooper, Lydia has told us all about you, please, take a seat." He said. The three of them sat beside the others and were introduced to the rest of the glorious creatures. The Elveens were called, Amadeus and Donatella, the pixies and fairies had a variation of cutesy names like poppy, petal, bubbles and Tulip, the dwarves had, what would be deemed ordinary names like, Frank and Simon, the centaur, who looked the least pleased to see the guys with a ferocious scowl aimed directly at them, was called Stan. "Lydia has offered to help us; will you do the same?"

"Yes, wherever our Lydia goes, we do too." Cooper smiled. Vinnie used ever fibre within his body to stop himself from rolling his eyes.

"What do you need from us exactly?" Vinnie questioned. Kalmin sighed as he stood, head of the table, looking at the allies big and small.

"Let me fill you in on what's happened in Crypskie."

6.

The peaceful and diplomatic land of Crypskie, had always been so glorious, so glamorous, it was home to many beautiful and elegant creatures, some beastly but honourable and living in harmony for years upon years, until one fateful day something got into the land, whether it was summoned or had travelled there of its own accord, it was a dover demon, a yellow eyed monster possessing the body of a human, it was not terribly troublesome at first, it would play tricks and cause 'bad luck' to happen, it would cause little harm and more mischief whilst playing along with its impish friends that hid in the land. Unfortunately, it then found a way to bring more sinful beasts unto the land, specifically more demons, vampires, werewolves, Taranions – huge tarantulas with lion heads, and Gashadokuros – vile skeleton people whose main goal consists of biting off heads, predominantly human and drink their blood like water. These monstrous beasties tore through the land, abolishing what they could, causing destruction on every path they took, slaughtering thousands of peaceful beings and families, making the survivors run away and hide in safety. The Crypskians as they were known, that subsisted the slaughter had been hiding for such an extensive time, they even tried to fight off the bad guys, but regrettably it was not a huge part of their nature, therefore, they lost more of their loved ones and had to send for others, usually from other realms, to help.

"So you see, we need all the help we can get, those that have been to help haven't stayed and those that came taught us how to fight with magic, unfortunately, magic doesn't always work on these beasts, we need to learn how to fight the old fashioned way, and go into battle." Kalmin explained.

"We are going to win back our land!" Stan grunted.

"We can help for a short amount of time, but our world needs us, something bad is going down." Vinnie said. Kalmin nodded.

"Lydia has explained it all to us, we appreciate any help you can give."

If their lives were an action packed, full-throttle, fight to the death kind of movie, this would be the part of the fast paced, good times mixed with bad times montage; they started their first lesson in a room within the ever expanding building, it was a huge empty room, decorated in the rose gold theme the rest of that place seemed to have going on, and it was dotted about with mirrors along the walls and across the ceiling, enough space for many and enough view of their own reflections to learn the right moves, to learn defence, to learn how to fight. Every creature, big, small, beautiful and those with faces that only a mother could love, stood before Vinnie, their tutor, as he explained the art of true battle, the eternally deep fear that builds within your passion, the blood pumping adrenaline that can cause the silliest of actions or the bravest measures, the sheer pain that comes from the injuries and damage you could be dealt, the loved ones that could be lost, and that feeling of guilt when doing the damage and doing the killing that can manifest within ones soul, even though you know you are doing what needs to be done. Once the main speech had been entertained, Kalmin brought in swords, and other handheld weaponry, and Vinnie showed them how to swing the blades, to swipe and swish and put your full body weight between each manoeuvre, he showed them how to smash, even with the wrong end, were they to find themselves in difficulty and most importantly, how to block attacks. He showed them how to move, elegant, like a dance, swiftly, side to side, back and forth, rocking, ducking, diving, and evenly distributing body weight like a boxer in the ring, anticipating the enemies' next attack whilst trying to stop them from anticipating their own. After the initial trial, he then allowed them to have a go at fighting each other, without the fatal part of course. It took it's sweet time, it took days in fact, Vinnie, Lydia and Cooper watched as the beautiful beasts fought each other, swiping, ducking, diving, clashing, almost taking each other's heads off, there were a few minor injuries, nothing lethal, nothing a cause for concern. He then moved them onto much smaller blades, consisting of items such as, knives, rocks, axes and hammers all of which, after the sword fighting, the creatures were quick to learn. Stan, the gruff Centaur, was very good indeed, he could wield a blade or weapon of any proportion with ease, but he was brutish and lacking in empathy, he was also absent in the ability of following orders, he was hell bent on his own prerogative, he had even caused harm to some of his friends, although apologetic, he was fond of the ruthless way he could be when readying for a war. They then moved onto bow and arrows, in a different room this time, it was what could only be described as an indoor – outdoor, it was made to look exactly like a forestry, targets sat at one end, the pleasant creatures exerting their bows and their arrows at the other, Amadeus, Donatella, Stan and Kalmin were the first four up, pulling back their bows they let them spring forward and if you were close enough you could hear the melodic whistle of the rapid arrows as they rocketed through the air, all four hitting a target, Amadeus and Donatella's, as if professionals, hitting the bullseye whilst the other two hit their targets just not as central. The fairies, Poppy, Tulip, Bluebell, Pot and Weed were not quite as good, no amount of manual target practice was working for them, but sneakily, they used a little fairy dust and their arrows hit the targets more on point. The dwarves, now they were good which came as a surprise to them all, Frank, Simon, Billy and James hit the targets, although not with bows and arrows, but with their sharpened, heavy axes. The pixies, Mud, Bubbles and Petal, were no good at all, their abilities were limited due to their tiny physiques, even their magic was less than mediocre they would have to stick to the spells they could fathom.

After what felt like an entirety of weeks, the magical beings appeared to be ready, or at least ready enough not to die in a one-sided blood bath.

Around the meeting table once more, the beasts, jolly and full of pride, clearly gave the impression that they were now prepared for the long winding battling road ahead, it would be them who would make their move first on the bad guys as an element of surprise, the story of the good ambushing the bad, locked in a battle to win over the world in which they loved, and Vinnie agreed they were in good form to do so. The creatures he taught went on to teach all the others in hiding around the land, giving the impression that the terrestrial had an ample amount of an army to take on the militia of brutes.

"And we raise our glasses for the help unduly needed, to Vinnie, Lydia and Cooper, friends we have found in these three, may we go on to win back our land and – " Kalmin was stopped short with his glass raised in the air when, Tiko the multi-coloured Cockatoo flew into the room.

"They're coming," It squawked. "They're coming!" It flew around the room in a frenzy. "They're attacking the lunar village, the community under the sea has already fallen!"

"This is it," Kalmin shouted as they all stood from the table and made their way to the arms room, everyone started putting on their armour and collecting their weapons. "The battle begins."

"How far is the lunar village?" Vinnie asked.

"It is only up and down the pokey hill." Stan replied. The centaur was now wearing shiny black armour over his torso and a matching black helmet, in a holster was a vast sword, making him look even mightier than before. Vinnie would ordinarily feel intimidated, but in his mind he could only think of how confident and lacking in discipline the centaur was, he would be a good fighter, but he would leave his friends to die, Vinnie suspected, besides he had a mission to be getting back to.

"We will be seen making our way there, it is too out in the open." Amadeus said quietly, his voice idyllic like a song.

"What can we do, they need us in the lunar village, and we have to help." Frank said gruffly.

"Kalmin, is there another way to get there, even if the distance will take longer, is the hill it?" Vinnie asked.

"No, the hill is by far the quickest way, but there is a forest that can bypass the hill, but as I say, it is the much longer route."

"So, let's split up, a group of us one way, a group the other, we can't all go one way if we'll be easily spotted, we can use that old cliché of the element of surprise if one group faces the bad guys first." Vinnie strapped the last of his armor on and holstered his sword, he also opted for his gun and blade that nestled nicely in his new weapons belt. He looked quite the part, or so he thought.

"Sure, grand, you mean use the top of the hillers as bait." Stan grunted. Kalmin sighed.

"Of course, he doesn't mean that Stan," He thought for a moment. "Yes, it's a good idea, it'll take an extra thirty minutes or so going around the hill though, so those going that way will have to leave now – "

"And how do we choose who goes the less suicidal way, who's going to lead each group, do we go at the same time, what happens if one group gets there first?" A barrage of questions came at Vinnie and Kalmin from various beings, both men took a step back.

"I'll go up the hill, I'm quick, I can probably scope the bad guys out before they can take action, as I do, do this kind of thing for a living," Vinnie said, immodestly. "Lydia, Cooper and whoever wants to take the other route with them do so, and whoever wants to be my guest, it's totally your choice."

After some debate those deemed the strongest and the 'little bit' weakest were evenly distributed amongst the two groups, not all happy with their placement but accepting, and they set off, all of them completely unawares as to what way their fate would play.

The forest route was in actual fact called, 'Flor da Floresta' and for Lydia and the others it was a stunningly gorgeous canopy, the trees were tall, looming but magnificent, the leaves a multitude of intricate colours, like deep blues, popping pinks, and pretty purples, the grass was a funny texture, almost like turf and it was turquoise, there were signs of small wildlife, visually they saw the ones that fluttered by, they were bright, some even glowing, different types of flying insects, like butterflies, but wing spans twice as big, some furry, some even feathered, Lydia frowned at the thought of it all potentially being destroyed.

Vinnie led the others up the long, steep, somewhat rocky hill. The rocks present were shimmering, they had a silvery sheen that glistened like glitter, and the bushes were a bold and fiery red that seemed to wave at them as they walked by. Once they reached the top of the hill; the sounds of their gasps rang into the air, they could see the devastation before them. A much larger village, than the one they had previously been in, that went on for as far as the eye could see, was in absolute tatters. Buildings were crumbling, completely knocked down, still ablaze in a burning mass or just a pile of rubble.

"Right, I know this is a horrible situation, but we have to be brave, let's get down there, search for survivors and keep an eye out for the enemy, they may be gone, or they may be hiding or disguising themselves to ambush us, we must stay vigilant, be prepared for some awful scenes, I know it's not something you want to think about, but you may not expect what you may see." Vinnie shouted out to everyone. Taking in a deep breath, he led the others down the hill.

Slowly walking through the war-torn village, they could see

what acts of violence of which had occurred, the vehement bloodshed, the torturous agony, death. The bodies of the dead, creatures both good and bad, lay like sleeping troops, each sprawled in ways that indicated their way of death, all over the new founded battlefield. Lydia and the others joined them, their faces filled with shock and horror, and then they split into smaller groups to search the grounds. Vinnie, being the lone wolf he was, went off on his own, down an eerie alleyway, where two long. Crumbling, but still standing, buildings ran alongside each other. As he neared the end of the path, he could hear a crunching sound. It was louder as he approached, there was some gross sounding squelching too, and it was close. Rounding a corner, Vinnie stopped in his tracks. In front of him was a Gashadokuro, it was bigger and more frightening in the flesh, or not-flesh for that matter. It was a skeleton form, large, extra extra-large, human in shape but more like bear sized, it had two broken boned wings on its back, its wingspan bigger than itself, and it was covered in sticky blood. It was sat chomping on a body, using its massive teeth to rip the flesh away and chomp on the pieces of chewy skin, it had removed the head from the body and began drinking the blood from the remaining part of the neck and then continued chewing the remains. Vinnie bent to pick up a stick from the ground, as he did so he heard a growl, and before he knew it the thing was racing toward him, fast for a bag of bones, it dived on him knocking him to the ground, it was pure power and brutality, he held its face at arm's length as it tried to rip his face off. Barely able to hold it back, Vinnie grunted and grind his teeth as he bustled with the creature, using one hand he held its face from his, his arm becoming tired and sore, he used the other to stretch for the stick, almost cheering as he grasped it, kicking the creature in its non-existent Ghoulies, which apparently seemed to work as it fell back off of him, he jumped up and pulled a lighter from one of his pockets, the Gashadokuro dashed at him again, this time he expertly dodged the vile thing, flicking the lighter, willing it to ignite as he watched the flint spark, again the creature leapt, again he evaded skilfully, and to his joy, flash, the lighter flame danced, he lit the stick, immediately it caught fire, and slowly made its way up the wood, Vinnie continued to elude the creatures attacks, punching and kicking until the stick was fully alight, or enough not to burn his hand off, he then allowed the beast to dive toward him and as he felt, and smelt, its breath on his face, he shoved the fire through its lanky bones. It began to shriek and scream, backing off and flailing like a fish, every one of its bones began to ignite until it was a ball of fire, and as quickly as it caught fire, it became a pile of ash on the ground. Before he could congratulate himself on not dying, he heard clapping from behind him. He turned to see a woman, all in black leather, jet black hair but searing bright yellow eyes.

"Dover Demon!" He rumbled.

"You can call me Daeva," She laughed. She appeared in a flash right beside him. "It seems you know how to kill; you want to switch sides?"

"Not a chance!"

"Shame." She lunged at him with a blade, but he was quick off the mark, he had his blade out in time to clash with hers. They found themselves in a sword fight of sorts, jarring and banging weapons, kicking and the odd swift punch in between, but as the demon received a few cuts she did not play fair. She used her powers to force his body back into a wall, holding him there with an invisible force, a big smile plastered to her face. She tutted. "You didn't think I was going to have an honourable fight did you, I'm a demon, I don't play by honour, just deceit." She lunged at him with her knife that was quickly deflected by an arrow, Vinnie was immediately released as Daeva lost her concentration. Stan, Kalmin, Lydia and Cooper raced forward at the demon, Stan leading, having a horses backside certainly helped with speed. He threw holy water from a bottle at her, causing her to scream from the searing pain, he then wrapped a rope around her pulling it tight, she attempted to move but unfortunately for her, etched into the rope was spells of entrapment, specifically for demons, meaning she was unable to break free. As the others reached her, she screamed obscenities at them, she writhed and wriggled in the ropes.

"Shall we keep her as a prisoner?" Cooper questioned.

"No, demons are slippery, conniving beasties, she'll slit our throats the second she gets the chance." Stan said. She laughed.

"Or possess you." She winked. Exchanging glances with Vinnie, Lydia took a deep breath and stood in front of Daeva. Removing a cross pendant from around her own neck, she placed it in the palm of her hand and placed her hand on Daeva's forehead, immediately the demon began to scream in pain as the cross burned her head.

"Remove te a coram malo, quod humanum est, dimitteret unusquisque servum mentis, corpore et anima, post se relinqueret suum homo, et descendunt ad inferiora inferni, quo pertinent," Pushing the cross with more force, Lydia continued. "Ab hoc mundo, ad infernum, ab hoc mundo, ad infernum, ab hoc mundo, ad infernum!" The Dover demon began to squirm and screech, its head flopped side to side and its face began to distort. Lydia stepped back as Daeva screamed at the top of her lungs before her body gruesomely exploded, covering the friends and their surroundings in a vile yellow gloop. Lydia stared in shock, this was not how an exorcism usually went down, a normal exorcism, if there were such a thing to the average human, would conclude with a pained demon in the form of a coloured goo, leaving the body through mouth, ears and nose of its captive and a ring of fire burning from the ground would then drag the demon back to hell, usually leaving the host alive, or at worst dead, never before had any of them seen an exorcism end in explosion.

"What happened?" Vinnie said gruffly. Lydia shrugged.

"Maybe because we're in a different realm?" Cooper suggested. They all nodded in agreement. The rest of their troop arrived and Amadeus the Elveen, pulled out a large flask from the small canvas bag he carried, it was full of holy water. Everyone dipped and poured the holy water over their weapons, exorcisms take too long so death by holy weaponry seemed a better fit, especially if the hosts would not be surviving anyway. Before they could discuss their next move they heard a commotion coming from ahead, running to a more open area they discovered more Gashadokuros chomping down on the flesh and blood of other creatures, they were joined by vampires and the beastly Taranions, there was no element of surprise, and they had been spotted. That was it then, there was simply no turning back, on impulse the two groups ran at each other clashing with immense force. Some of the smaller soldiers eaten immediately by the Gashadokuros and Taranions. Lydia used a spell to bind a Taranions Legs with its own web as it tried to catch her, it fell with a great thump and she sliced its belly open with her blue crystal. Kalmin flew above them, gliding along and using his sword to chop the heads off as many vampires as he could along the way, Stan stampeded through the battle, his mighty legs and hooves trampling vampires and his sword stabbing at the Taranions, whilst many others stood back and shot the Gashadokuros with ignited arrows, their shrill cries could be heard as they burned to dust. It was little time before more Dover Demons appeared, six in total, three males and three females, all with glowing yellow eyes, and all hell bent on death, taking souls was their purpose after all. Vinnie and Cooper fought them together, their weapons sparking with the demons, one female contorted her body so awkwardly it did not look human anymore, Vinnie stabbed her through the heart, and she blew up, leaving that gloopy eggy gunk in the vicinity she had once stood. Cooper took two males on, one held Cooper whilst the other attempted to cut him, Cooper kicked him right between the legs, or in male terms - where it hurts, and swiftly flung his head back, cracking the nose of the one holding him who let go involuntarily from the force and its newly bleeding nostrils. Spinning around Cooper watched as the Demon he head-butted twisted his head around three hundred and sixty degrees with a massive grin on its face, he stabbed him, and that grin was gone, replaced by the gunk that one might produce when one has a nasty cold. The other male went for Cooper again, this time Cooper wasted no time in wasting him, dodging the attack he thrust his sword into the side of the demons head, and like that it was jelly.

Meanwhile, Vinnie was in battle with the last three, a male and two females, he had taken some blows, he had a bloody lip and some facial scratches, he was holding his own until he was kicked in the back of the legs by one of the ugly foes and he fell to the ground.

"Oringorgons, you think you can beat us, but you're weak." Said one of the females. Vinnie, swerved her claw like scratch and jumped up forcing his blade through her chin. And just like that, she died.

"Weak, winning, it's all just swings and roundabouts." Vinnie said. The other two charged for him, Cooper came out behind one and jammed his sword through the back of its head whilst Vinnie shoved his through the other ones chest. Poof, another gross substantial mess of substance unknown filled the night and ground. They could hear what could potentially be described as, 'a battle cry' from a not too yonder distance, and they watched in awe as more of the respectable guys joined the fight, they were survivors from other surrounding villages, they had been hiding in the forest from the attacks on their homes, waiting for either doom and gloom or a hero to save them, it appeared all they needed was a leader, a forefront to take a hold of and follow so they could immerse themselves into the action. Instantly, they began to help take down the number of depraved folks. The very depraved that were getting evermore angry at their falling figures, their roars, howls, growls and frustration rang out amid the skirmish. Taranions roaring as they ripped limbs off, leaving bloody appendages strewn across the fields and then roaring in anguish as they were axed, stabbed and punctured.

Lydia caught a glimpse of black and white in her peripheral vision, she turned to her look to her left, at her ten o'clock, there was a couple of men in suits Standing perfectly still, their heads tilted in a pose a dog might do when listening, and they just stared at the ongoing blood bath. She could not be sure what side they were on at first, they were well dressed, well groomed, no weapons, just themselves and a look of shock perhaps? That was until they gave the ugliest, dissatisfying, sinister grin, the kind of smile one of those unpleasant, haunted porcelain dolls might have on their evil little faces. And as Lydia decided they were in actual fact part of the corrupt crew, their bodies began to distort, and misshape, as if something was trying to push its way out from under the skin, their mouths grew longer and the surrounding skin began to break and tear, and shaggy grey fur started to appear where the skin used to be, their nails became sharp claws and their hands padded paws, their neat teeth now huge fangs – they were indeed, werewolves. In full wolf form they ran into the fight, howling at the top of their lungs, letting all who cared to listen and know that they had arrived. Tearing the flesh and bone from the creatures they caught, ripping out throats and organs with claws and snouts, they even ate some of the fairies and pixies whole like tiny little snacks. Lydia joined in this new fight, with the cutting off heads of these beasts, silver helped kill a werewolf but full head removal meant no chance of survival, and as they were relentless in causing suffering to all, she could not watch the slaughter of her newest allies.

The battle raged on for some time, tired, hungry, cold and injured, they fought bravely on both sides, and it only ended when the last howling wolf was slain, Vinnies blade the last to inflict the pain. Looking around as he wiped the blood from his hands, he took in the sheer devastation, it was like a sea of churning red blood, gloopy guts and stacks of bodies, the last of the Gashadokuro fires burned out leaving puffs of smoke to evaporate into the air, all that was left alive, was a very small minority of the moral people and all was silent, like in the eye of a storm, quiet, surreal, not even the tweet of a bird could be heard. The Centaur slowly trotted to the front of the troop.

"We won." Stan Shouted. And like a win at a home team's football stadium, the cheer of the winning crowd was loud and glorious.

7.

The celebratory dinner and party were a magnificent spectacle. Loud, proud and merry – the drinking kind. Everyone was in high spirits, they had won back their land, and although there was a lot to do to rebuild what was lost, the land was free of evil, and were evil to return; the good guys were battle ready.

"You can stay for longer if you wish." Kalmin told the friends with a slight slur to his speech. Lydia smiled, she had refrained from the alcohol, they had a long road ahead and she could not be dealing with the hangover.

"Thank you, but we have our own evil to conquer."

"I understand, you will be leaving in the morning?"

"Actually, we were going to slip out now whilst everyone was enjoying the party." Vinnie said. Cooper and Lydia rolled their eyes, 'party pooper' were their collective thoughts.

"We're staying until morning." They said together. Vinnie sighed, giving an eye roll of his own, he was not impartial to a decent party, but needs must, and the need of stopping a certain bad individual, or bad individuals from destroying the world was a must, and a must do yesterday in his eyes.

The party continued well into the night, it was a show of happiness and drunkenness, defeating an enemy one had thought to be much more powerful gave a euphoric feeling to all. Vinnie, feeling drained, left the festivities and went to 'his' room, that he had been allocated. Sitting at the end of the bed he closed his eyes, just resting them, and found himself thinking about the past. Thoughts flooded his mind about his child hood, his mother and father, they were Oringorgons too, people destined to 'save' others from monsters, to absolve and work with the imperatively 'good' ones, they became friends with Lydia's and Cooper's parents, it is how the three became the best of friends, they went to the same school and then often saw each other outside of it too. Their parents were habitually on the road so the three would stay with 'Uncle Clayton' not a real uncle, but a man so close to the family he was never seen as anything other than family, who would often tell them stories of their parents skirmishes, like the battle of the smoke people, deadly things, they could get through any crack, they could suffocate and even possess people, the only way to remove them was trapping them in something air tight. After days of fighting smoke with leaf blowers and vacuum cleaners their parents captured and buried all the smoke people that had wreaked havoc on a poor town, in little boxes they created themselves. Another tale was the wolvenbeast carnage, the vile wolf/bear like creatures had been on a huge hunt and set about killing hundreds of humans in many cities, Vinnies dad had single handily taken out a vast majority of them after his wife and friends were abducted. Vinnie remembered the huge wolvenbeast tooth his dad brought back for him, it was gone now, lost when he was around sixteen, in one of his teenage rebellious manoeuvres he threw it into the mouth of a kraken, but that is another story. He recalled the first beast that ever attacked him, without his parents but in the presence of Lydia and Cooper, they were in actual fact at school, a huge old building, once belonging to royalty, so incredibly old fashioned and full of nooks and crannies, and they had snuck out of their maths class, not for any particular reason but simply for the sheer fun of it, their primary objective; snooping around forbidden areas of the school. They found themselves in a very old, dusty, crumbling library with a very hungry sludge monster inside. It was massive, its body glistened from the oily and black slime, which oozed out of him as he moved, and leaving a trail everywhere he went. It had two giant white eyes and four sword like teeth in its mouth, it had arms and legs, but they seemed to disappear under the gross goo. It had tried eating them, it had tried slashing them, they fought back, they eventually used an aerosol can and a lighter to set it alight and ended up burning half of the school down. Those were the days. Hearing a scream, Vinnie jolted up right. Disorientated, he jumped up and retrieved his weapons, hearing the shouting and banging about he soon realised it was not a party that had just gotten out of hand. Running back to the 'Party room' he was shocked to see the combat commencing inside. There were more vampires, werewolves and vampidnas but this time there were Blemmyae, things with the body of men but no heads, just faces in their chests, they used strange wooden swords with thorns sticking out of them to batter the good guys. There was also a pride of Chimeras, creatures with a head of a lion at the front, a head of a goat in the middle and a snake head at the end of their tails, they were breathing fire all over the damn place.

"Vinnie!" Lydia shouted as she raced over to him, chopping a few heads off along the way.

"How'd they get in?" He used his gun, shooting several of the Chimera heads.

"I don't know, it's like they came from nowhere, we were ambushed."

"There's too many of them!" Cooper barked in husky form, he ripped the throat of a vampidna out and joined the other two. They continued to fight, watching in horror as many they fought beside were being slaughtered, dying painfully in pools of their own blood.

"Guys if this is it I – " But Vinnie did not have a chance to finish, in a sudden flash a blue and white glowing, swirling vortex of some sort appeared in the wall behind them, dragging Lydia into it, Cooper returned to his human form and grabbed her hand, but the portals pull was too strong, it was taking them both, as they lifted from the ground and floated toward it Vinnie grabbed a hold of Cooper's foot, digging his heels into the ground in an attempt to keep them from being taken to god knows where, but he was dragged along the floor like a petulant child. Kalmin and Amadeus tried to help but before they knew it the five were thrust into the portal and landed in a heap on a cold wet floor. They were no longer in Crypskie, they were no longer in another realm, and they were back on the 'normal' dimension of earth. Standing up and brushing themselves off the five looked around.

"We need to get back!" Kalmin said, realising they were no longer in his realm, he focused his energy on turning his wings invisible for all to see.

"There'll be nothing and no one left." Vinnie replied.

"Vinnie!" Lydia exclaimed.

"I'm sorry, but why beat around the bush about it, it's the truth, there were far too many monsters, too much power, our friends didn't Stand a chance, they were all drunk and merry, everybody is dead, you know it, I know it – "

"You don't have to be that harsh – "

"He's right," Kalmin sighed. "I could see it in Stan's eyes as I was sucked through that thing, he was dying, they all were, but why were we saved?"

"More importantly, where are we?" Cooper studied their surroundings. It looked like a small town or city, lots of houses, shops, a cinema, restaurants, he thought he could see a mall in the distance, but it was very dark, there were no street lights on and more relevant; there were no signs of life, it was like a ghost town. Catching a glimpse of something in his peripheral vision, he noticed what looked like a human shape on the floor. He nudged Vinnie who indicated that he had also spotted the being, he took a few steps forward. It was a person, oddly, they were crouched on the floor with its back to them.

"Hello?" He said gently. No response. He cleared his throat. "Excuse me?" He said louder this time. The person suddenly lifted their head. Turning, as if in slow motion the gang saw its face, and their facial expressions quickly turned to shock. It was a male human, once. It had flesh torn from its face, an eye protruding from a socket, the hair had been ripped out in places leaving bloody, wounded patches, its jaw was much lower than it should have been, and it was covered in another person's blood, the person it had been eating. It was a zombie.

"Ah shit!" Vinnie groaned as the zombie snarled, jumping up, faster than he had anticipated, the moving remains ran at him. He quickly took it down with a clean-cut head shot. Before the five had time to process they heard in the distance the sounds of stomping feet and a fleet of groans. Looking ahead they could see the hoard of the undead running toward them, any ordinary day it could have been a civilized group of runners doing a marathon, however, the blood, the guts and the half-eaten corpses said otherwise.

"Let's get to the mall!" Lydia shrieked. And the five high tailed and ran in that direction.

"Why is it always a mall?" Vinnie moaned.

8.

The hoard of hungry, man, woman and child eating flesh bags, were incredibly quick on their mangled feet for the usual undead, their gangly limbs not holding them back, as Vinnie and the gang raced across dead roads, vaulted over fences like Olympians, and cascaded through peoples gardens, the undead began to catch up with them, with only one thing on their rotting brains and that was the living flesh they would love to sink their teeth into. Amadeus and Kalmin, still wearing their holsters, pulled out their swords and took off some heads when the gainers got too close, those heads rolled but they remained groaning, the bodies left searching for their vital missing parts, another oddity, considering dismembering a 'normal' zombie would usually cause complete bodily shut down. Vinnie managed a ton of deadening head shots before running out of ammo, Cooper and Lydia had no choice but to just run, run, run. They got closer to the mall, it looked derelict, haunted, but also locked. Cooper and Lydia pulled on the closed doors just to be sure, they bashed on the metal shutters, tapped at the windows, and made incredible amounts of noise in order to stir anybody hiding inside so they could enter the building, with no response they had to find their own means of entry but there was no way in without smashing some very thick glass and unfortunately, that would defeat the object of getting away from the zombies, as they would also be able to get in any holes made.

"We'll hold them off for as long as we can, but you have to find a way in," Vinnie shouted. "Use some of your bloody hocus pocus Lydia!"

"Right, right." She gulped. She watched as the undead approached Vinnie, Kalmin, Amadeus and Cooper, the four now using blades and swords to slice and dice pieces of the rotting flesh, the zombies trying to bite and scratch, whilst the guys stabbed them in their brains before moving onto the next. Lydia pulled a book of spells from her bag and flicked through, her mind racing in a bid to figure out what spell she could use, stopping on a section devoted to disappearing things or people, she made her choice. Finding the spell, she then took some chalk from her bag and drew a symbol on one of the doors, made of glass, like an infinity symbol, but squarer, inside of a large triangle.

"Anytime now Lydia!" Cooper shrieked as he dodged a flesh eater whose head was sliced in half by Vinnies blade. Lydia held her hand in front of the window.

"Vitrum evanescit ineamus." She said. The symbol gently glowed white and in a flash, the glass disappeared. She squeaked with excitement and checking the book again, she whistled to the other four, who, after defeating more of the undead, ran through the new entrance one by one. Vinnie was the last to enter. "Propinquus nunc, Speculum reditus." Lydia said and at the precise moment a zombie reached the hole the glass reappeared, leaving the zombie a bloody mess all over the window.

"I wonder how long the glass will hold." Amadeus whispered.

"Who, the fuck, are you?" Came a voice from behind them. Turning, they saw a group of people, all appeared to be living humans, all carrying weaponry, such as butchers knives, cleavers, guns, shotguns, shears, baseball bats, golf clubs and more. The man at the front of the group, the one with the angry voice, was somewhere around fifty years old, greying hair and beard, wearing jeans and a checked shirt, and he pointed a fierce looking shotgun at the friends with an expression on his face that can only be described as that of ferocity.

"Um, sir – "

"Lydia?" Came a female voice from the back. Stepping to the front, a woman with a pretty face, wearing a long purple dress, with shoulder length curly black hair and tanned skin smiled at them, a familiar smile which beamed in fact.

"Lacey!" Lydia shrieked. Running into each other's arms the women embraced.

"Lacey, long time no see." Cooper laughed. Lacey hugged Cooper and reluctantly gave Vinnie a handshake and nodded at the two newcomers.

"They're okay Jack." She said and the group lowered their weapons. "Lydia is my sister."

The new group of people were friendlier and less guns blazing, once all the pleasantries were over and done with, sitting along the benches and tables within the malls middle section, where the food court was, they all ate and drank whatever was on offer, still clutching their weapons for fear of imminent attack. Lydia explained to her sister all that had happened and what their goal was, to stop the rising of the king of beasts. Lacey too had heard the rumours, she had been doubtful of their truthfulness, until the living dead began their decent of destruction, getting rid of the big beast was indeed high on the agenda, and of course she would help, but only once they rid the town of zombies, she had been living there for several years after the death of their parents and had grown to love it.

Lydia and Lacey were 'enchanted ones' essentially witches in the modern world, but better known to be 'pure of heart' meaning they use their powers, spells, and enchantments only for the greater good, some call them white witches, but the word 'witch' often has bad connotations to it, as the vast majority of what would be known as a witch, were actually called 'Hexhers' or the male variant 'Hexhims' and they were known for being incredibly wicked, hell bent on causing havoc and doing evil of which enchanted ones were the complete opposite. The sisters had once had a huge family, four brothers, two more sisters, many aunts, uncles and cousins, but other than one brother and a couple of cousins, they were the only ones left, the 'enchanted ones' were taken out by many of the bad Hexhims and hers in a combat of magic. It was not the beautiful rainbow coloured blow out people may envision when hearing of a magical battle. It was full of evil, angry and grotesque beings fighting the very placid enchanted ones, wands were used for quick spells that caused immense harm and death, curses used to inflict slow pain, the usual weapons, knives, swords and guns made their appearances too, but not held by hands, slashing through the air of their own accord with spells meant for killing. Not many of the 'enchanted ones' made it through that fight, some but not all. The sisters were convinced that there were more out there, hiding away with their families in a bid to survive. If it were not for the Oringorgons help, there would already be a world with much less good in it, and many monsters roaming the streets, hiding in closets and under beds. Lacey explained their current situation.

"The local graveyard was covered in a thick white fog, some of the resident youths who find hanging out there 'cool' felt the earth shaking and then these mud mounds appeared, before they knew it newly animated human corpses began climbing out of their tombs. The towns people have done their best, we all fought, bravely, there's been a lot of fatalities though, and by that I don't mean dead, but undead. It looks to me as if these zombies have instructions from whomever their resurrecting buddy is; to only turn humans into them with bites and scratches as opposed to eating them alive, they aren't as easily killable either, although you've probably discovered that for yourselves."

"Oh, Peachy," Vinnie shrugged. "And how many do you think are out there, because from where I was running there seemed to be quite a mass?"

"A hundred, maybe two at a guess, and I hate to say it, but that glass isn't going to hold for very long." They all looked over at the horde of misfits bashing at the big glass doors, it was heavy duty stuff, but these zombies seemed awfully stronger than you would expect, strong magic reanimated those cadavers.

"Wowzers, this is going to be fun." Cooper chuckled nervously. Kalmin and Amadeus were communing with a few of the towns' people, calming the crying mothers and children mostly.

"So what can we do Lydia, I've tried the return spell, I've tried disappearing spells, I've tried the making us a portal to safety, I've even tried enchanting this whole place with protection spells, nothing is working, either I'm rubbish, which is an absolute farce, or they're not your ordinary zombies as we'd already guessed, so what do we do, I can't let these people here die, I've lived in this place for so long now, they're my friends, they need me, how do I save them?" Lacey looked worn out, down and like she wanted to give up, but the people she cared about were keeping her motivated. Lydia let out an exasperated sigh.

"I wonder if there are witches nearby, Hexhers or hims like this kind of destruction don't they, it's right up their alley, they'd likely be the only ones powerful enough to hinder our magic, especially if they can predict what we'd try to use to counteract," She shook her head. "We have to stay safe as long as possible, if the zombies do get in, then we're going to have to fight, hold them off as long as possible until we can get people to safety."

"But surely more will just come," Lacey shrugged. "We'll all die."

"Not if we use our magic together to hold them off as long as we can, we fight the ones that get through – "

"It's suicide!" Jack, Lacey's friend said sternly.

"No, we're not going to do nothing, I have a plan, if Lacey and I can locate the one doing this with a location spell, we can put together a hex for Vinnie and Cooper to find and use on them and then well, they'll have to kill them." Lydia explained. They heard a load snap-like noise and as they all turned to look, it appeared the glass was already weakening. There was a large crack going down the length of one of the glass doors and another few smaller cracks on some of the others.

"I can't believe this magic shit!" Jack groaned.

"Did you believe in Zombies before today?" Cooper asked. Jack shook his head. "There you go, you learn something new every day."

"It's as good a plan as any, let's do it." Lacey agreed. Vinnie nodded. Kalmin, Amadeus and Jack agreed to help fight alongside the rest of the able bodied townies were the undead to break through, and by examining the cracking glass, the impending doom of zombie infestation was imminent.

9.

Lydia and Lacey stood over a round, metal table with a large map of the town in the very centre of it. They lit four white candles and placed them around the map. Lighting one last candle, Lydia held it directly above the centre of the map. Lacey placed Lydia's blue crystal and her Green one either side of the map, unanimously they both began to glow. Clearly, Lydia said;

"Adiuva nos quaerere si unum invenio, qui maledixerit in una villa et in plateas, ubi est ens, quod habet dominium omnium monstrorum medio producta blasphemia." Tipping the white wax it suddenly turned red as it hit the map. The crystals joined together and followed the wax until it stopped at one point and disappeared. The crystals pointed at a small farmhouse.

"And there, my friends, is our frenemy." Lacey winked.

"That's Barney's place, he died a few months ago." Jack sighed.

"Okay, so get this hex together then and we'll – "Vinnie was interrupted by the smashing glass of the main doors. It was sudden but not totally unexpected, considering the mass of ugly decomposing miscreants on the outside, the zombies began their ascent to munch all of the malls current living occupants. "Shit!" The townspeople, Amadeus, Kalmin, Jack and Lacey picked up their weapons, like soldiers going to war, they were ready if not afraid of the many possible outcomes of such a fight.

"We're relying on you guys." Lacey said, a grimace more than a smile upon her face, as the group charged the undead. It was a mass clash. Zombies heads came off with unearthly groans, limbs were severed, some of the nice town folk were bitten and flesh ripped down to the bone, exposing their insides not unlike an interactive science lesson, only this would turn the living insides dead, and the dead would arise living, what an unscientific mind fuck. "Come on!" Lydia growled, and Vinnie and Cooper followed her out along a corridor, through a little trinket shop and out of a well-hidden exit, something Lacey must have told her about, Vinnie thought. Lydia collected some stones, some sticks and made a little slit on her finger causing it to bleed slightly, she dripped one tiny drop of crimson on a cloth that she pulled from her bag and wrapped the sticks and stones up in it. Chanting something that the guys could not quite catch, she handed the sticks and stones to Vinnie.

"Throw this at the bad guy, say loudly, Captionem, they will be temporarily trapped and you need to douse your blade in holy water, again, then stab them in the heart, it is the only way you can insure you kill them, this zombie outbreak isn't a virus it's a curse, so when the magic bearer dies, so do they."

"Right, Okay." Vinnie nodded.

"Aren't you coming with us?" Cooper asked.

"No, I need to help my sister, you'll be fine," She smiled. "Now what do you have to do?" She looked at Vinnie.

"Throw the thing, say craptonium and stab 'em with holy blade, got it." He replied. Lydia shook her head.

"Throw it at them, make sure it touches them, anywhere is fine, say Captionem, and stab them, say Captionem?"

"Captinotion, caption, captain – "

"Captionem!" Lydia shouted.

"Captionem, captionem, captionem!" Vinnie said. Lydia let out a huge sigh.

"God help us all, good luck!" And she disappeared back into the carnage of bodies, bites and rolling heads.

"Captionem, captionem, I got this."

"We got this." Cooper agreed, although the uncertain look on his face said quite different. They were not searching for long as they quickly found their destination, it was a lovely little blue coloured farmhouse, on an equally small field, that obviously had once held many a farm animal, it, in that moment, appeared to be deserted. They approached with caution, practically on tip toes, blades at the ready, hex device in hand, prepared for an ambush as they crept up to a window and peered inside. It looked as if no one was there at first, but then they spotted the dancing shadowy glow of a minor blazing fire coming from a back room. Skulking to an open window a little further along, the two friends climbed into the kitchen as quietly as humanly possible, which was until Cooper unwittingly knocked a cup from the kitchen side, Vinnie attempted a superhuman mid-air grab but instead hit the cup harder causing it to shatter into lots of tiny pieces. Cringing the two waited for the consequences of breaking and entering, but no one came. Slinking through the kitchen, the two looked around the corner into the next room, there was a little fireplace, complete with pirouetting fire but no beings present.

"Upstairs?" Cooper whispered. Vinnie shrugged. They crept into the living room. Suddenly, they were thrown to the other side of the room by an invisible force, Vinnie smashed into a bookcase and landed on the ground with a ton of books falling on top of him. Cooper was pressed against a wall and held there, feet levitating above the ground. Looking up, Vinnie spotted the greying hair poking out of a black hood and the shrivelled face of a Hexher who was staring at Cooper with devilish eyes, he knew it was a Hexher due to the star symbol carved into her forehead, ordinary witches and of course enchanted ones, did not have those. She began chanting some gibberish whilst holding Cooper against the wall with her power. Vinnie jumped up and threw the hex thing at her, it flashed and went up in a grey smoke.

"Campmodium," Vinnie said. The Hexher laughed. "Ah shit, Craptomium, capa-fuck it!" He ran at the woman who held out her hand and he immediately stopped in his tracks unable to move, she made one forward motion and again he was thrown across the room. Cooper had been released as her attention had gone to Vinnie and he was now in husky form. He dodged the Hexhers attempt at stopping him and dived at her, chomping down on her hand like his life depended on it, she screamed then shook him free with an almighty strength Copper had not anticipated.

"Suffocant!" She yelled, pointing her fingertips together her eyes seemed to smile as she watched Cooper's dog form struggling to breathe.

The zombies were relentless, some of the townspeople were being eaten alive, whilst Lydia chopped off the heads of those trying to gnaw on her, and she could not help those dying. Lacey, Kalmin and Amadeus sliced and diced like warriors and many of the townspeople were giving the living dead a hard time too. Punches and kicks were not doing the trick, but one hell of a battering from a baseball bat, and a beheading via garden sheers was certainly doing the job. There were many of them though, and not enough of the good guys, as Lydia decapitated one zombie, whilst stabbing another through the cheek, then turned to dismember another, she willed that Vinnie and Cooper were doing their part, and not getting killed, or she would kill them herself.

Whilst Cooper was slowly being strangled, Vinnie ran at the Hexher like a rugby player. She dodged him but released Cooper in the process. Cooper coughed his breath back and the Hexher turned to Vinnie holding her arms up and making fists she gritted her teeth.

"No one gets one over Helena," She put her arms forward. "Exprimi animam suam." Rapidly, Vinnie felt a searing pain in his chest, as if his heart was being squeezed with a vice. He tried to breathe but he could not and began gasping for air. Cooper, feeling dizzy snuck up behind Helena.

"Its always the ass." He whispered with a huge sigh. Growling, he widened his jaws and bit her as hard as he could on the backside. She squealed, letting Vinnie go as she swivelled around facing the other way and grabbed Cooper by the snout. Vinnie coughed and spluttered up what felt like his guts, and although he was incredibly disorientated, he got straight to his feet and holding back no mercy, he jammed his holy watered blade through Helena's back, pushing it in further and further until it went straight through her heart. She screamed in utmost agony and within just mere moments of the attack, she became a pile of ashen-grey dust on the floor. Cooper sneezed several times from the dustiness, before reverting to his human form again.

"Congratulations on forgetting the word man." He frowned. Vinnie clutched at his chest.

"I solemnly swear to listen to Lydia from this day forward and forever," He said. "Just don't tell her."

It happened so abruptly, it felt to them all as if time had just simply stopped, everything went totally quiet as a bright white flash caused the fight to suddenly halt, nobody could see anything in the blinding glare, many closed their eyes from the searing eye pain it caused, some of the living even wondered if perhaps they had died without realising and were now going toward the light in a bid to reach their paradise. However, as quickly as it appeared, the striking flash was gone. Looking around the crowd of bloodied, yet living people, they realised the fight was over, a cheer rang out amongst the crowd, the zombies had appeared to have disappeared, no doubt those already dead had returned to their graves, but the bodies of the fallen remained lifeless on the ground. Lydia let out a huge sigh of relief, they had done it, she thought, they got the bitch that caused all the mayhem, good on them.

She would not have to kill them herself after all.

10.

The townspeople were incredibly grateful of the friends, again, going out of their way to help those in need. They were fed, watered and given beds for the night to freshen up, ready for getting back on the road and on with the mission.

"I slept pretty well considering we almost had a zombie apocalypse." Cooper said with a mouthful of eggs and bacon. Lydia grimaced at him talking with food in his mouth.

"Me too, but we have to get on, we need to get the vial to Intention and get the keys location, for all we know the bastard beasties have already found it." Vinnie sipped on his coffee. Lydia nodded.

"I'm sure they haven't, or we'd know about it now, but it doesn't mean they're not closer than us."

"What will happen if he does rise?" Lacey asked. She sat beside her sister holding her hot drink tightly in her hands. Lydia frowned. Cooper swallowed and stopped eating.

"Probably the end of the world." Vinnie said, matter of fact.

"Really?" Lacey gasped.

"No," Lydia sighed. "We can fight back, even if he pops out of the ground, we have many people who will help to stop him."

"You're very optimistic Lyds, but, he's very powerful, he was basically the god of the monsters, he's worshipped, he will probably be able to resurrect some of the worst things that you can imagine, we're only human, some of us with a little more talent, but human none the less, this is a fight we'll likely lose."

"Well thanks Vinnie, you miserable dick!" Lydia stood and left the kitchen, stomping like a child as she exited. The others looked at Vinnie.

"What," He shrugged. "It's true, but I'm optimistic that we'll get the key first."

"I know what you're saying, but there will be just as many good guys wanting to live as bad guys wanting to take over the world, if, god forbid, that motherfucker lives to see the light of day, we'll be ready to take him and his minions down!" Cooper growled, he was always the heroic voice of reason. Kalmin and Amadeus stood in the doorway nodding in agreement, Lacey looked unsure and Vinnie laughed.

"Okay friend, better to die trying than die a wimp I suppose."

When the friends were ready to leave, they bought two vehicles from the local car salesman, as sad to lose their parents as they were, and as much as they wanted them back, the inheritances they received from their untimely deaths certainly made their jobs easier, and they packed a range of supplies of which the townspeople offered, such as medical supplies, food, drink, and the odd bit of weaponry. Vinnie, Cooper and Lydia went in one vehicle whilst Kalmin, Amadeus and Lacey went in the other.

"I'll be back soon!" Lacey shouted as she revved the engine. Waving at the souls she was leaving behind, she followed the others who were already accelerating at speed, hurtling away, and Lacey thought to herself as she sped after them 'I hope I will be back one day,' but her sister needed her help and she was determined to be there for her, family was everything after all.

Lydia had her foot down on the accelerator, the road was wide, open and practically empty so her and Lacey had a little race to lighten the dreary mood. As Lydia drifted around a smooth corner, Lacey was close on her tale, Lydia stamped her foot down harder and the car shot off like a bullet, her sister struggling to keep up whispered something under her breath, and as Lydia's car chugged and came to a stop, Lacey zoomed passed her. Lydia sat open mouthed at the audacity of her cheating sister. Starting the car again she raced after her, feeling both angry and competitive, until suddenly a child ran into the road. She swerved and skidded, narrowly missing the boy before coming to another stop. The three friends looked back to see if the boy was okay, but he was gone.

"Did I hit him, did I hit him?" Lydia said frantically. All three scrambled out of the car and searched the general vicinity. Vinnie shrugged.

"You didn't hit him," He said. "He just vanished."

"Was he real, I mean, we all saw him right, but was he, maybe, a ghost?" Cooper questioned.

"Possibly." Vinnie nodded. Lydia shook her head.

"I looked straight in his eyes, he was alive," She said. "I think he was in trouble – "

"Oh no, you're not starting that shit again Lyds, we have, so far, got nowhere with stopping the bat shit crazy king of beasts from being let out of his grave, or cage or whatever the hell is keeping him from destroying the planet, because we keep detouring with helping others, now don't get me wrong, I'm a good Samaritan and all that, but I'd rather stop the whole world from needing our help than a lost little boy, harsh but he'll be in much more danger if we don't get to Intention soon." Vinnie explained. They heard a car approach and pull over beside theirs. Lacey got out of the car.

"Are you okay, I'm sorry, I didn't mean to – "

"It wasn't you Lace, there was a boy in the middle of the road and now he's gone, I sense that he needs our help, but Vinnie wants to leave him." Lydia told her sister who gave Vinnie an evil look, the kind of look a mother may give to a misbehaving child and he took a step backwards, eyes widened, a slight fear emanating within him of retaliation from the angry enchanted ones.

"Well, Vinnie isn't going to run off on his own is he, I say we help the boy." Lacey smiled. The others agreed, Kalmin and Amadeus shouted their pacts from the car, they were like sheep, after all, Vinnie scoffed. Vinnie threw his hands up in defeat with a huge sigh. His mind ticking over, wondering why he ever though he could lead the leadless.

"Fine, there was a sign for another town back there, let's go and see what they know about a missing boy." He said through gritted teeth as they all got back into the vehicles.

11.

"Ha ha, Buttsweep." Cooper giggled as they parked outside of a pub, it appeared to be the local pub, based on the lack of other drinking holes.

"It's Buthesweep actually." Lacey corrected him. The town was nice, quaint, but something was absent there, it felt almost low-spirited, like something was sucking all the joy away and leaving behind sadness, the people that they passed all seemed very unhappy, even to the point their skin had a slight bluish-grey tinge, dull, losing the will to live, it was as if the town was held against its will in a great depression. Entering the pub, called Buthesweep Lions, they noticed that everyone inside sat solemnly, almost silently drinking their beers, barely making conversation or eye contact with each other. The six of them found a table and Vinnie went over to the bar. The barmen looked up from the glass he was cleaning.

"What can I get you?" He asked quietly. Vinnie ordered some beers as one does in such a place.

"What's going on here, why does everyone seem so?" He paused.

"Lost?"

"Well, I guess that's one word for it, it's so quiet, it's the middle of the day, this little town should be up and about surely?"

"It used to, not so long ago in fact," The barman shook his head. "But things have changed, bad things have happened, this town isn't what it used to be, far from it, some things ruin a community."

"Like what, you can tell me?" Vinnie questioned. The barman

looked into Vinnie's eyes for just a split second before he seemed to acknowledge an honourability within him.

"It's just, this place," The barman sighed. "This picturesque little town holds a terrible secret, and it's taken its toll on the residents." Vinnie leant in as the barman beckoned him over. "Have you noticed there are no children?"

"Well, I can't say I did actually, but we've only just got here, and we've only driven through a small part of the town, but I suppose, no, there were no children."

"Some say it's a curse, others the bogeyman, but something is taking our children, they're disappearing, and we've had search parties, police, and other authorities from other towns, but they have just vanished without a trace," The barman explained. "It's like they were never here, like they never existed, and no one is doing anything about it, the people here have given up hope." Vinnie sighed, of course, he thought, this was a job for Vinnie and the gang, why was Lydia always right?

"Okay, I'm sorry to hear that, but you're in luck, we will help you find your kids." Vinnie said. The barman smiled, not a happy smile, but the saddest one Vinnie ever did see.

"You're welcome to try," He said. "But they're gone."

Back outside, of which he marched his troop, Vinnie explained the situation to the others, the goings on in the town of sorrows, without the laughter of children.

"Damn, that's depressing, I also really needed a drink." Cooper Moaned.

"So, I don't think I quite understand, their kids, their flesh and blood little humans, have just been disappearing, poof, without a trace, and nobody is doing anything about it, zilch, nada, fuck all?" Lydia gasped.

"Apparently they've tried, but there's no trace, no proof that the kids even existed other than empty bedrooms and old faded pictures, outside of this town the kids do not exist, authorities have been and gone and think these people have lost the plot, this place is fighting on its own."

"So, where do we start if we've got nothing to go on?" Kalmin asked.

"I guess, we can start by interrogating the town, find out about the kids that have gone missing, exactly whose kids have gone missing, what sort of time frame that has passed between each, uh, let's call them abductions, whether the parents are into anything dodgy, if there were any strange occurrences or unexplained phenomenon they've seen or experienced, you know, if there was anything significant that happened around the time they started disappearing that could point us in the right direction as to where these kids have gone, and anything else you can think of in the case of missing children." Vinnie suggested. The others agreed.

"Okay, it'd be easier if we split up, cover more ground, more people?" Lacey proposed.

"Good idea, I think in twos though, we don't know these people, I mean, call me paranoid but they could be making it all up and turn out to be people eating giant lizards or something." Cooper chipped in. The others looked at him with curiosity, or perhaps the looks were pitying his foolishness, he had odd thoughts a lot and he often voiced them without filters.

"Let's do it." Vinnie nodded.

Cooper and Vinnie, Lacey and Lydia, Kalmin and Amadeus were their little teams, cross-examined as many people that would allow them to. Going from home to home, store to café or restaurant, they managed to collect some information, and it appeared that there were around twenty children missing, ranging from three years old to thirteen. Vinnie and Cooper went back into the pub they had first stepped into. Approaching the barman again, Vinnie introduced them.

"Keegan," He replied. "You're really going to look for them, call me cynical, but no one has found a trace that our kids even belonged on the planet, who died and made you Sherlock?"

"It's what we do, and I'd be honoured if you called me Sherlock," Vinnie replied. "Is there anything else you can tell us?" Keegan sighed.

"My son," He swallowed. "He was the first to go missing."

"We're sorry to hear that." Cooper whispered. He could see the pain in Keegan's eyes, it was both an emotional and physical torment, ripping into the very heart of a man that had probably once been tough and no doubt his son's idol.

"He's five, Jack, he was such a lively little boy, loved playing and reading, he had a very vivid imagination," He paused, obviously picturing the little boy in his mind as an aggrieved smile briefly crossed his lips. "He was a little fearful though, he kept saying there were monsters under the bed, in the closet, under the sink, no amount of reassuring would calm him, I had to go through this whole ritual every night of checking for monsters." Vinnie and Cooper exchanged glances. Monsters, now that was their forte.

"And, I suppose you never found anything?" Cooper wondered aloud. Keegan raised an eyebrow.

"Well, obviously not," He sighed. "My brother came to visit us, and he was always the eccentric, spouting tall tales of swashbuckling adventures, a load of made up bullshit of course, but Jack loved it, and my brother used to bring all these stupid gifts from his travels, trinkets and other rubbish that he collected as he never stayed in one place for too long, and this last time he brought back this book about bogeymen and read it Jack, before bed of all times, and from that moment on, Jack was afraid of the dark, afraid of the shadows and the monsters that he thought were there, my fucking brother turned my brave boy into a scared little shell of the boy he was before."

"You talk about your brother in the past tense?" Vinnie said.

Keegan nodded.

"After that last visit, He had read Jack the book, I remember listening and thinking it was a rather strange book, I still have it actually, it has funny textured pages, I don't know what it's made out of but it's not much like paper, anyway, he read it and said he had to go, it seemed so abrupt, as if he suddenly had a sense that he had to be elsewhere, he refused to stay the night, even after I tried to convince him, it was late and he was clearly exhausted, but he left, then, that night he, he, he fucking crashed his stupid fucking car and died, just like that, gone, probably up there gallivanting with the angels whilst I mourn his ridiculous death," Keegan paused as he pointed to the ceiling then slowly lowered his hand to the other, rubbing them together as a kind of comfort, he closed his eyes in thought. "Shit, silly bastard, then it was around three days later, that my boy, my Jack went missing, fucking gone, without a trace." He let out a huge sigh and dropped his head into his hands.

"Okay, thank you Keegan, we're sorry we've had to ask such personal questions, but truthfully you've been a great help, I need one more thing from you though, would you mind getting me that book, I'd like to have a look at it, it sounds interesting?"

"Yes, I suppose, I don't think a book of bogeymen would help you find my son though."

"Still, you never know, it could hold some key evidence, or it could be nothing, I'd like to follow all paths, a new set of eyes could find some new information."

An hour later the six of them met back where they had left the cars, just outside of the local pub. Vinnie stood, leaning against his vehicle flicking through the 'freaky' book Keegan had given him. It was undoubtedly not the sort of tale any innocent child should be told, it had an aura to it, just a simple touch had Vinnie feeling uneasy, cold, his mood darkened, he shivered as if someone had walked over his grave, it also had an odd texture to it, kind of like skin, smooth in some areas and rough in others, the front cover depicted a slight 3D image of a black leathery hand, with remarkably long fingers and jagged sharp nails, the tale the book told, was an interesting one indeed, it depicted the bogeyman or men, Vinnie had heard many different fictions about 'the bogeyman' over the years, each one with a similar pattern that went along the lines of; a creature, somewhat human like, although with monsterly differences, that usually scared or terrorised predominantly children, the occasional adult, but children were the 'believers' so the 'bogeymen' could conjure up a fright to satisfy their needs, this one was not all that dissimilar, but it was one Vinnie had never heard before. Instead of just being a story about a creature that frightens children when they disobey their parents, it was a story of 'bogeymen and women' who kidnap children, starve them for weeks, keeping them alive with just fluids and a little bit of dark magic, until they are skinny and fragile and then feast on their bony, dying bodies, leaving not one trace of the children that were once there. Vinnie shuddered, this would have put the heebie jeebies into him as a kid, the 'bogeyman' was one story his parents had told him was not a real apparition.

"There's not a lot of info to go on is there?" Lydia shook her head. She had a downcast look upon her face, the kind that made the rest of them understand the seriousness of the situation, with her accrediting sense of danger, the others knew this may not go in their favour, and they could see the strain the situation was putting on her.

"Actually, I think I've sussed it." Vinnie held the book up for them to see. "The bogeyman, or bogey peeps in this case." Cooper laughed.

"That's a book, the bogeyman was just a monster in a tale that parents told naughty kids to get them to tidy their bedrooms, I mean, mum always said this one really was a load of bollocks."

"Or so we thought." Vinnie replied. Lacey took the book and flicked through it. She frowned and let out a long, over exasperated sigh.

"You, as much as it pains me to say, might be right."

"Really?" Lydia read over Lacey's shoulder, Vinnie scowled and rolled his eyes at Lydia's blatant treachery. "Yes, that's it, the kids started disappearing a couple of weeks ago, every parent we spoke to, said their child was afraid of monsters under the bed."

"Or in the closet." Kalmin said.

"And then they disappeared without a trace, as if they barely existed." Amadeus exhaled.

"So, what do we do, where do we go from here, where did they come from, where did they go and more importantly, how do we get those kids back?" Cooper questioned. His canine sanities making him a little overzealous.

"Well, I can tell you where they came from," Lydia said. "They came from the book." She tapped the cover. "This book is made from human skin and bone, probably the bodies of the bogey people, so when it's read out loud, specifically to children, it's like they have permission to come and take the children, it says in here that they stash the children underground to starve them, so chances are they're still in town, and the kids are probably still alive, but they won't have long left."

"They're below us?" Cooper asked. "Sewers?"

"Possibly, that or if there are any caves or mines in the forestry around here."

"And how do stop them, these bogey things?" Kalmin enquired.

"I guess the return spell would work, magic works against these things better than weapons." Lacey chimed in. She handed Vinnie back the book.

"So, we split up again, and we find these bastards and get these people their kids back!" Vinnie shoved the small book into his coat pocket. "And then get on with our actual mission!"

12.

Lydia and Lacey took to the mines, they were just on the outskirts of the town and they appeared completely abandoned. They were dark, a little wet and extremely dusty. They were confronted by some spiders, a few oversized crabs and a frightened cat, of which they attempted to rescue only to get hissed and swiped at, they soon decided the cat could fend for itself. Down another one of the tunnels, Lydia quickly came to the conclusion the children were not there, there was not a single speck of evidence that human life, or otherwise, had been down there for a while.

"I don't think there's been anyone here for a long time, we're wasting our time, these kids haven't got long left, and we can't afford to make the wrong decision." She said. Lacey agreed.

"You're right, we should turn back and catch up with Cooper and Vinnie, and pray they have found the kids already."

"Yes."

Kalmin and Amadeus were searching the local woodland, it was not quite a forest, it was too small to be called that, but it was full of thick, tall trees, bushy shrubs, a few boulders, and surprisingly very little wildlife, there was nowhere for bogeymen to hide children for any length of time. The two discussed the probability of them finding the kids there and came to the supposition that they were wasting their time and decided to meet up with Vinnie and Cooper.

Cooper ran at his full capacity, feeling momentarily carefree as the wind tousled his fur, along the picturesque little beach that sat just beside the town. It was a such a beautiful setting, the sun was shining like a beacon, the glistening, soft sand was warm against his doggy paws, and the elegant waves crashed against the shore causing swirls of white horses amongst the blue. Vinnie's eyes nearly rolled all the way to the back of his head as he stood at the entrance of the cove waiting for his muttly friend to finish his canine capers.

"There really is something just a little bit wrong with you, you know that?" He said as Cooper re-joined him in human form, a small smile, still present across his lips.

"Ah, come off it, I wouldn't be me without my quirks, you wouldn't have me any other way."

"I would." They entered the little cove with borrowed torches that they shone ahead of them, lighting up the gloom, leaving an eerie cast of dancing shadowy silhouettes along the rocky walls, they walked slowly, their stride small and calculated in a bid to remain undetected, were anything on the prowl, and what started as sand beneath their feet, soon turned to uneven rockiness, they found, what they believed to be just a small cove, was in fact turning into a vast cave. It seemed to go on for miles upon miles, the torches could not find the end of it.

"Perfect place for hiding some child snacks." Cooper shuddered, his mind wandering to that of poor defenceless children succumbing to a monsters feast. He took just a few steps forward and halted suddenly. "Look." He directed his torch at a small red coloured toy that lay face down on the gravelly floor, instinctively Vinnie picked it up, sensing no danger around the little plush. Turning it to face him he realised that it was a little red devil, not the evil king of hell kind, but actually, kind of cute looking, with big black eyes, a curly pig-like tail, teeny horns and a tiny soft pitch fork, there was no mistaking that it was indeed a child's toy.

"This has to belong to one of the missing kids, I'm not sure if that's a good thing or a bad thing though."

"What, in case they're already, you know?" Cooper gestured slicing his neck, dead. Vinnie let out a deep sigh because that was exactly what he was thinking.

They continued through the never-ending cave, taking more cautious, quiet steps and lowered their heavy breathing, the two friends had equipped themselves with guns that Vinnie had conveniently stored in his jacket of tricks.

"I think I can hear something." Cooper tilted his head. "Yes, I think it's a child crying." Cooper went back into Husky form and ran in the direction of the noise. Vinnie close behind. The cave went on for miles and it appeared to drop, going deeper and deeper into the gloom. As they approached a large archway, they ducked under it, and Vinnie could hear something too.

"I think, I think I can hear it, crying, I hear it too." He whispered. Cooper slowed to a trot, Vinnie tiptoed, and the sobbing was closer. Walking further into the damp, shady cave, Vinnie lifted his torch up and immediately spotted the children. Several children of varying ages lay in small concrete jails, like cages but made from stone. Some were unmoving, others sobbing, all looking malnourished and weak. Devastatingly, they could see from where they were stood that a few of the children were no longer breathing. Vinnie and Cooper, Cooper now in human form, headed toward the children.

"We're here to get you out." Cooper said. He stopped abruptly in his tracks, Vinnie did too. They both heard a very strange, almost ear piercing, scraping noise, like fingernails down a chalkboard, followed by a low, droning noise, as if someone was humming from the back of their throat, and they deduced that it was coming from behind them. Turning, they recoiled in horror. There were three looming figures in front of them, two were huge creatures, spider like bodies spindling with eight legs, half of it covered in fine pointy tufts of black hair, the other half was covered in shiny, yet rough scales, they had three vicious looking heads each, one of a slithering snake, one of a rabid wolf and one of a disfigured man.

"Shit!" Cooper squealed. Vinnie remembered the tales of the Sniploms, they were supposedly creatures not unlike the one in front of them, although he could not recall the disfigured man, and they preyed on and ate shifters, because a shifters power gave strength to the three different featured creatures, but Vinnie also remembered that Rory, Cooper's sadly deceased brother, reveled in telling that particular bedtime story, just to scare the hell out of Cooper when he was a little kid, Cooper, at the time, was a gullible child and had believed them to be real, but Rory, who was fond of Vinnie and his blatant moody scepticism, had told Vinnie in secret, that they were completely made up entities from his own wild imagination, and he had enjoyed making up such scary creatures, for the torturous fright of his little brother, and true to the tale, many a night, Cooper had lain awake, afraid of being torn apart and eaten by a Sniplom. So why, pray tell, was there a fake beast, two in fact, very real and in front of their persons? If Vinnie had not seen them with his own eyes, he would have teased and joked Cooper about it for the rest of their existence. Vinnie turned his attention to the third figure, and suddenly, he felt Ice cold, like he had been drained of life, like hope had vanished and disdain took its place. The other figure, tall, impending and frightening, was of a grotesque skeletal appearance, it had a very large, disproportioned head, with discoloured horns protruding from its forehead and sat upon the head, was a raggedy top hat, behind it's frame it had an enormous wingspan consisting of bony parts and what looked like ripped fabrics, and in one of its large gaunt hands was a cane with a dark blue sapphire stone set into the top of it. It was he, the King of beasts, or how he was described in the books and exactly how Vinnie had pictured what his foe would look like. The two friends were only momentarily paralysed and perplexed by the situation, because although feeling overwhelmingly scared, they had to believe in themselves, they had to be motivated, there were children's lives at stake, and they were betting on the boys. They pulled out their guns quick as a flash and began shooting at the fierce beings, who screeched and yelled like banshees, but the bullets had no merit, for they went straight through them like they were flickers of what was but not what is.

"What the actual f - "Cooper dodged one of the sniploms as its eight legs rapidly jumped at him, it was fast and agile on its many limbs, the three heads whipping this way and that, biting out at him trying their very best to catch some flesh to grind between their teeth. Realising the gun had no effect, Cooper placed it back into his pocket and he whipped out a lighter in an attempt to set the creature alight, because the friends had a few mottos and 'if all else fails, burn it,' was one of their favourites', but again, the flame, just like the bullets, proceeded to go straight through the vile monstrosity like it was ghost. Vinnie lashed out at the boned man, refusing to believe it was the actual King of Beasts but instead some sort of projection, and at the other Sniplom with his mighty blade but like before, it passed through the beasts like they were not even there. He, however, was punched straight in the stomach and felt the pain sear through his body as he was sent flying into one of the children's prisons. Cradling his sore stomach, Vinnie stood up.

"Mister," Whispered a sweet voice from one of the cages. Vinnie turned to see, softening his hard expression as his gaze focused upon a boy so frail and nearing death, Vinnie recognised him, he was the boy in the road, the one they had avoided hitting, he must have escaped the monsters and had tried getting the friends attention, but the creatures were fiendish and had managed to scoop him back up again, they were prolific and set on retrieving what they desired. "They're not what they seem Mister, they're not what you see, they're what you're scared of." It was like a light bulb moment, of course, Vinnie understood. They were not there at all, at least the creatures they were seeing were not. Running toward Cooper, with a slight hobble from his sore stomach, who was being held down by a furry spider leg and narrowly avoiding getting eaten by the three heads, Vinnie pulled the bogeyman book from his pocket. As soon as the creatures saw it, they withdrew and returned to their original forms. Long, lanky, grey and bald, with no eyes but a mouth full of pale yellow teeth and long sharp fingers, they were the former bogeymen, and true to form, they take the form of your biggest fear, and Vinnie's biggest fear was not the king of beasts himself, but the King of beasts rising and potential power he had which could bring an end to the world. Cooper, realising his fear was in fact just a fake, jumped up and swiped at the creature closest to him, its body distorted and twisted until it was back to normal again. The other two bogeymen rushed at Vinnie, almost floating on air they were so fast, grabbing his wrists he could feel them burning, so much so the book flung from his grasp and onto the floor. He fought, struggling with the creatures, but their grip on him was just too tight. Cooper jabbed at the other bogeyman, but he too was restrained by the strong force, it wrapped itself around him and began to squeeze, he felt cold, and breathless, and he felt as if all the joy was slowly seeping out of him, he was sad and fearful. As the two friends began to feel like all hope was lost, they heard the voice of a saviour.

"Oh no you don't!" Lydia swiped the book from the ground. "Back you go, bitches!" Opening the book it began to glow and Lydia lifted it into the air like Rafiki did with Simba, then there was a sudden blast of cold air, a tornado like vortex began to swirl out of the book, it was mesmerising, the cave became a blustery, cold, damp and noisy mess, the ground shook and the friends watched as the bogeymen fought to stay away, fought to prevent flowing into the swirly mass, but the force of the tornado dragged them ominously towards the book, Vinnie's captors released him against their will, they clawed at the ground, leaving trails of scratch marks as they were dragged toward the book, Cooper's imprisoner held on for only a few seconds more before it was prized away, and was powerfully hauled into the book, disappearing with a screech, the other were yanked with incredible energy after their vanishing friend, the book instantaneously flew from Lydia's hands and landed with a thump on the floor, the tornado whirled around, getting smaller, and smaller, until it was a tiny whirlpool, then it died out, and the book closed of its own accord.

13.

The children were incredibly weak, frail, they were most likely mere shells of their former bright and adventurous bubbly personalities, as Vinnie had noted by the towns' people, there were a small number that had unfortunately perished, their tiny, lifeless bodies unable to cope with the malnourishment, and perhaps even the turmoil of fear itself. The six friends immediately helped the living children out of the cages they were captured in, and true to their word, they carried back the bodies of those that had sadly passed on to the parents that had been searching for their children in vain. They led a slow, depressing walk back to the town, in a sorrowful silence, they reached the road stopping briefly to catch their breaths, they continued until they reached the pub, stopping just outside like an army of the damned. Keegan stepped out, his mouth was open wide in shock and disbelief, his eyes were teary, and he and his son raced toward each other for the biggest embrace, a missing son, found again. It was not long before the other parents and carers were out and scooping up their beloved with affection and joy, their gratitude toward the friends made known, even for the bodies they brought back, despite the families being devastated for their losses, they had their loved ones to say goodbye to. They all accepted that something had been amiss, once the children had gone missing, the families, without help, had believed their babies would never come home, dead or alive, they blamed themselves, wishing they had listened to their babies when they told them there was something under the bed. Hindsight, is a wonderful thing.

That evening, in an honorary display to be proud of, they

watched as the families whose little ones had perished from child abductors as they were led to believe, set the bodies off, in gorgeous little handmade wooden boats, to sea, setting them alight as they pushed them away from the shore, the tide taking them out, their bodies and bones burning for their souls to be set free and move on from the cruel world. They set off a spectacular display of fireworks and made the loveliest of speeches, and despite it being a difficult and distressing situation, they found it also to be a celebration of the lives and joy those few children had, missed, gone, and never forgotten. Vinnie and the gang said their goodbyes to the nice folk of the town, he knew they would never forget them, although he anticipated the king of beasts rising, there would always be faith and people who would be willing to help, to put their lives on the line in a bid to protect their loved ones, and even strangers, and that faith would keep the world on turning. And now they had to have faith enough to stop the bad guys from causing ruin.

Back on the road again they did not race this time, in fact, Vinnie and Cooper drove opposite cars, to avoid that whole debacle again. This time they were not going to stop until they reached Intention's place.

As they approached the long road, named 'Stretchy way' perhaps, as it was a very long road indeed, on their way to Intention's humble abode, coincidentally, both vehicles began to cough and splutter, as if they had caught the same sudden illness. Then, like magical parallels, their tyres popped, and both skidded to abrupt halts.

"Mother of fucking hell!" Vinnie growled as he got out of his car, slammed the door with gusto, and checked the front tyre, the wheel was punctured alright, and as he checked the boot, his language was much more colourful, the spare tyre was also punctured. "We're going to have to pile in with you Cooper." He shut the boot and looked over at Cooper who was inspecting the boot of his vehicle. Cooper shut it and grimaced.

"Umm." He shrugged.

"What?" Vinnie said angrily. His face was flushed red with frustration and his fists clenched at his sides. "The front tyre is punctured, and the spare is – "

"Also, fucking punctured, because that's our shitting luck, absolutely, mother fucking peachy." He said through gritted teeth. "It appears someone doesn't want us to make it to Intentions." He crouched beside the front drivers side tyre of the vehicle he was driving, inspecting it, feeling the anger rise as he noticed something that most definitely, did not belong in a tyre wall. He pulled out, with great difficulty, a large star shaped blade, it looked like a throwing star, something you could imagine a ninja might use when in combat. He held it up for the others to see. Cooper showed him the matching one from his car.

"They really don't."

"Looks like we're walking along Stretchy way then," Lydia and the others got out of the cars, retrieved all their weaponry and prepared for a trek. "Good exercise I guess."

"Exercise," Vinnie shuddered. "I'd rather eat a burger."

They began their long distance walk down the lengthy stretch of road, it was bumpy, gravelly, ominously dark from the tall, looming overgrown trees, it was also very quiet, quite eerily so, that it was apparent something out of the ordinary was going on, it was a gut feeling that lingered within all of the friends, an uncomfortableness that came from within all of their instincts, and it was unshakeable. Vinnie watched the trees like a hawk as he walked past, they seemed to grow ever thicker, closer together, and uncharacteristically vast as they strolled, and as he turned to look along the other side, he was sure something was watching them, eagle eyed and stalking, something was there in the shadows, lurking, awaiting the moment one of them falls behind, so it could pick them off like prey. Not on his watch. Vinnie veered away from the group and entered the shadowy trees; he expected a game of hide and seek but it was direct and surprising that the creature immediately attacked. It was tall, with greying skin, and patchy ginger hair, it had sharp yellow teeth and grubby, broken fingers, Vinnie believed this to be a wendigo, considered to once have been of human origin, but starvation crossed with a curse causing the human to become a cannibalistic monster, feeding on humans for its very survival. It aggressively pinned Vinnie to the ground with one of its grubby hands, but Vinnie was able to shimmy his knife from his belt, grabbing it, he shoved it through the wendigos chest, it screamed in pain and attempted to chomp on Vinnie's face, before it had the chance, Kalmin, who seemed to have appeared from nowhere, chopped its head off with one swift swipe of his almighty blade.

"Let's not go off on our own." Kalmin said as he helped Vinnie to his feet, re-joining the others he noticed the stern looks on all their faces.

"What, I had a feeling we were being stalked." He rolled his eyes.

"How about you tell us next time." Lydia huffed. "All we need, is the one guy that's supposed to help stop the potential end of the world, snuffing it to a bloody wendigo!" Vinnie shrugged. "I can handle myself." Lydia raised her eyebrows and sucked her teeth in annoyance. "Okay, point taken, Jeez." Vinnie sighed.

The walk felt never ending, with their legs beginning to ache and their belly's grumbling, they thought it was just going to go on and on and on, but alas, the end of the road came without more life threatening dangers to their surprise, and frankly, sooner than they anticipated, however, they quickly realised that it was still going to be an incredibly hard and exhausting rest of the journey to the Intention's lair. It was practically a mountain at the end of the road, not a hill, not a small ascent, but a huge, ginormous, beast of a mountain, and at the very top, Vinnie knew, was Intentions home, they would have to climb and walk along the tiny paths and edges like little ants, only very exposed and somewhat vulnerable to attacks at various angles. The cars could have only driven them so far anyway, it seemed. Vinnie sighed, he had not considered how difficult it would be to get to her home, he had been before, but via magic, her magic, no one else could get there without hers that way, so they would potentially die, just to get her a vial, and get them a piece of information. Why could she not have been kind enough to do it over the phone? Vinnie stared up into the abyss of mountain-ness doom. "Peachy."

14.

From the get-go, they knew they were in for a bumpy ride. The second they stepped on that mini yet looming mountain, things began to decline rapidly. They were confronted by werewolves, wolvenbeasts, vampires and Vampidnas, and a battle ensued. Vinnie used both his gun and his blade to shoot the heads and chop off the heads as brutally and briskly as humanly possible. Cooper became his Husky dog alter ego and ripped some throats out like a rabid animal, Lydia and Lacey used their enchanting crystals with spells to maximise the damage done to the beasts, and Kalmin and Amadeus fought like the brave soldiers they were surly becoming. It was like a set from a movie, the fight scene a hideous violent sequence of rage, dancing doggedly with weapons, fists and teeth, and a gory ending of bloody defeat, defeat of the bad guys that was. Blood spattered and feeling the brunt of the fight, the friends remained vigilant as they continued their ascent. Luckily for them, the mountain was not quite the mountain it first appeared to be, it was in actual fact, more of a very large hill that they had thought it was not, with large heavy ledges and a path, the illusion was to deceive but the reality was not as bad as it seemed.

"I'm hungry." Cooper sighed. His stomach growling with perfect timing. Vinnie agreed, patting his stomach like a child.

"I'm sure Intention will have food." Lydia rolled her eyes. "There's more pressing things going on in the world in case you hadn't noticed."

"Sh." Cooper said as he tilted his head to listen. He could hear a buzzing noise not that of a bee or those annoying buggers known simply as flies, but an inconsistent, multi-tonal buzz, and it was just ahead of them. He held up his hand to stop the others, of which they obliged, and he took one step forward, he stretched his arm forward and both his hand and arm disappeared, he pulled his perfectly intact arm back to his side. "It's some kind of, portal, vortex or alternate dimension maybe, I'm guessing Intention hasn't made it easy for anyone to make it up there."

"Swell." Lacey shook her head. "I suppose we better get on with it then." She did not wait for anyone to test the waters as it were as she pushed Cooper out of the way and walked straight through the invisible wall, and into the other place, wherever it was. The others exchanged glances, shrugged and quickly joined her, suspecting something to go wrong but instead coming out of the other side intact. Looking around they were in some, kind of jungle, it was very blue however, the trees and plants were dark greens and cool blues and the sky was a navy colour, albeit lighter than a night sky, the ground, almost of a fluffy feel but looked like glass, was a very pale, baby blue.

"Well this is a tad weird." Vinnie walked on, following the inadvertently obvious path the grass led them, and the others close behind. It was just a small trek before their ears heard the sounds of distress.

"Help, help!" Came a voice from up ahead. Breaking into an instinctive run, the friends raced to find the source of the danger. It was a woman, in a long black dress, her hair bright red like a fiery mane and eyes matching the surroundings of a deep ocean blue, she was trapped in a net, suspended above the ground, and it was not attached to anything, just floating there, like a balloon. "Get me down." She called to them as she spotted the friends just a few feet from her.

"Where are we?" Vinnie asked as he cautiously approached her.

"The blue." She replied, eyeing Vinnie with as much prudence. "It's not the nicest place, no matter how pretty it looks, there are things here that'll beat you, torture you, eat and kill you."

"Peachy," Vinnie gently used his blade to cut her out of the net. When the hole was big enough, she jumped down, Vinnie catching her before placing her down gently. "What are you here doing here, how did you get here, seems an odd place for someone on their own?"

"I was on my way to the home of a Gyporer, She's called Intention, she told me to bring her a vial of vampire blood, I'm sure being in a place like this you've heard of the king of beasts, and the possibility of him being brought back to well, take over the world with his monster minions, and well, I wanted to help stop it."

"Are you an Oringorgon?"

"Yes," She smiled. "Are you one too, are you on the same mission, are you going to Intention's too?"

"We are," Lydia said, suspicion crossing her features. "She wanted us to bring her something too, but she never mentioned anyone else or that she needed anything else, she's very secretive, how do we know you are who you say you are?"

"Well, I guess you don't," The woman shrugged. "But there's many of you and one of me so, you could take me down easily." Lydia thought for a moment, softening her features and nodding. Lacey Agreed.

"Why don't you join us then," Cooper suggested. The others nodded. "More heads are better than one, right?"

"Okay," She agreed. "I'm Eiddwen." They all introduced themselves and not a moment too soon as a loud screech rang out ahead of them.

"What, the fuck, was that?" Cooper shuddered. They vigilantly crept forward, weapons at the ready, prepared for the suspected fight ahead. Quick as a flash, ungainly creatures emerged from the trees. They were strange indeed, human shaped things, with a blue - grey skin, googly eyes, massive, bucked teeth and overgrown claws, they were also wearing loin cloths, Tarzan style.

"Oh, that was the fuck." Cooper and the others were not initially sure how to take on those beasts, they did not appear to assault immediately, but Vinnie led the others in an attack at full speed in a bid to get the better of the beasts. Running at the creatures, weapons waving, the things reciprocated, they all collided, punches thrown and blades stabbing, the creatures however, seemed to be unaffected by the blades, they went straight into them, like slicing through lemons, and left behind small open wounds that shone out a blue light, but there was no blood or even any indication that the things were in any kind of pain from the blows. They were strong, and they fought back with their huge, 'wolverine' like claws, swiping whilst the good guys dodged, ducked and dived in a struggle for survival. Kalmin angrily yelped and gritted his teeth as he got a seemingly painful slash to the face, leaving behind a deep cut on his cheek that dripped crimson red blood, furiously, he stabbed the thing that hurt him in one of its eyes, jabbing ferociously, like a man possessed, and it screamed in agony before its blue body glowed and unexpectedly exploded, like a bomb leaving Kalmin covered in a cerulean glowing goo.

"The head, that's how you kill them, stab them in the head!" He shouted at the others mid fight. Lydia and Lacey fought two back to back, swerving their talons and slicing with their crystals, helping each other where needed.

"Duck!" Lydia shouted at her sister, who immediately obeyed, and as she ducked down, Lydia jammed the crystal into the skull of the creature leaving both sisters covered in the blue stuff. Lacey then twirled around her sister and as the other creature attempted to go for Lydia, Lacey stabbed it in the back of the head and watched with a cruel satisfaction as it burst into a mass mess. Amadeus, who had finally allowed his wings to become visible again, and Cooper, quickly took down three between them, popping the suckers like bubble-gum using their weapons. Vinnie and Eiddwen faced two each, four ugly beasts that seemed bent on the take down and kill. Eiddwen had a funny shaped blade, it was long and curled at just one end, almost what a scythe may look like but on a much smaller scale. She was very quick, her fighting skills were exceptional, and she punched and twirled, evading and leaping, avoiding attacks whilst perforating her own. In no time at all, all the beasts were taken down, leaving a slushy blue, sea like mess behind.

"Well that was something," Cooper let out a big sigh of relief. "Something gross anyway, I'm tired, I need to rest, and all this fighting has my bones creaking." Cooper yawned.

"Ha," Vinnie shook his head, patronisingly. "No time for sleep now my friend, this isn't just fighting monsters mate, this is, to put it bluntly, stopping a possible apocalypse, we can rest when we've succeeded, or when we're dead." Cooper huffed, but agreed the mission was an important one. They reluctantly continued through the melancholy world and as they reached the end of the jungle, they passed through another invisible wall, slowly, they entered another dimension, it was different to the jungle, this time they stepped foot on a beach, sand at their feet, shimmering water in the distance, but the sky was a deep blood enflamed red. The most prominent thing there, in fact the only thing there, not too far in the distance, was a colossal golden pyramid that sparkled in the red glow. It appeared to be the only place they could go from there. "I guess that's our next destination," Vinnie groaned. "I hate Intention, she's clearly very paranoid."

15.

Lydia gently peeled open her eyes, it was dark, with only the flickering, fire lit torches, giving off a bouncy illumination and making the shadows dance around the gloomy room like freaky little gremlins. She felt groggy, her eyes heavy, her body ached, and as she tried to move, she heard a clunk and felt the restraints, she was chained to a concrete column. In front of her she saw movement, and she quickly noticed the gross beast that held her captive. It was half rotten human bones and half an unpleasant, raggedy cloth, its eyes pure white, it appeared to have no flesh, but it smelt increasingly like rotting skin, she recognised the foul beast from those Egyptian tales and Hollywood movies, that it was a mummy, she knew, being an enchanted one, that they did really exist, but she had never had the displeasure of ever facing one before. She gasped as it approached her, smiling with its skeleton face, looking directly into her eyes she could see the monsters intentions, because as it stared at her she found that she could not look away and the whites of its eyes began to show her how it would take her flesh and wear it, it wanted its body back, but it would need to do a human sacrifice first, very ritualistic, mummies were. She forcibly closed her eyes, a pain radiating in her eyelids, to stop the images, and she whispered to herself, praying that her friends would get there in time.

At first, they all stood along the shimmering shore, taking in with an awed admiration, the peculiar sights of the crimson sky reaching the navy ocean, it altered the colour on the surface to a beautiful plum shade. It gently twinkled and sparkled like glittery stars; iridescent waves crashed against the speckled sand.

"This is bizarre, remarkable, not something you see every day, but yeah, pretty weird." Cooper stated. The pals nodded in joint union. As he gazed out at the pretty sea, he was sure that he had spotted something out of the ordinary in the distance. "What's, what is that?" He squinted his eyes and gawked out at the deep briny sea, watching the rippling splash effect that appeared to be heading toward them. They had their arsenals at the ready, just in case.

"Ah, it's Anahita." Amadeus whispered, a smile, albeit small and somewhat sad, crossed his lips. As she advanced, they could see her more clearly, she was a beautiful, majestic mermaid. She had long flowing emerald highlighted hair, her skin was very pale, practically as white as snow, her lips were a pallid blue and her fins, or more precisely, her tail, that met her human form in the middle, right at the stomach, was a glossy shade of turquoise. She was a spectacular sight, considering Vinnie and Cooper had never seen an actual, living mermaid before, they had been told about her however, she had chosen to be female, after originally being born a male, something extraordinarily fantastic with mermaids was, they could change their sex whilst young whenever they pleased. She reached the shallows and waited for them to wade out to her, their clothes wet to their waists.

"Anahita, I thought Glaucus under-sea village had been destroyed?" Kalmin hugged her and introduced everyone. The pleasantries were short lived as she let out a deep sigh, a frown furrowing her sleek, shimmery forehead.

"Yes, tragically we have lost our village, may the souls of the departed swim in the sea sanctuary afterlife, there is but a small fortune, there are some of us left, we have been searching for you, I used a small portion of our magic and it brought me here, now I realise the magic must have known you would be here, I was here long before you, swimming in this, beautifully odd sea." She explained.

"Why, we can't breathe underwater, we'd be no help, and we can't take anyone back to Crypskie, everybody, everybody is dead, they're gone, can you find somewhere to hide, to be safe, I want to help, I really do, but we're already in a dangerous situation?" Kalmin questioned.

"I understand that of course, the human realm is our benign gamble, any other realm is much more monstrous, but the humans, they're rather unaccepting of our existence, our presence would cause quite the stir, I'd fear they'd attack purely out of fear, so, if we can find somewhere there to hide perhaps it's all we can do, all these other worlds, they're being taken over by beastly things, unimaginable monstrosities, of course all in wait of their king, we need the king stay down as much as you guys, if he doesn't rise, if we can stop it, we may get our homes back," She paused. "We want to help, not hide, when we're all healed, and the most vulnerable are safe we'll help wherever and whenever you need it, and guys, Crypskie may be dying, but some of its residents are not, I can assure you, Donatella, some of the dwarves, Stan, they're still alive."

"What, but I, I thought," Kalmin gasped. "We have to get to them!"

"We're kind of in the middle of something." Vinnie reminded him. "And I hate to break it to you, but the human realm as you call it, is also being taken over by monsters, you'd probably not even be noticed if you went there, strange things are happening to people and it's only going to get worse."

"Yes, but as it stands at the moment, it is the least affected, believe it or not, and Kalmin whilst I comprehend that you want to get to your friends, I think it would be much more efficient if we come to you, once you've made it out of these lands, wherever they are, we will find you, and help wherever we can, we must stop the worst from happening and we can do that if we all work together, I will tell the others I've found you, and that you're alive and well, and here take this." She said. She turned to Vinnie, distinguishing that he had taken on the leadership role, and handed him a long pearly shell with a hole in one end. "Blow on that when you need us, and I'll be able to find your location, recovery won't take long for us magic folk, but we need somewhere to hide in the meantime." Vinnie studied the shell, it was small at one end, larger at the other, a lovely stripy pattern in white and pale pink covered the whole thing, it had a smooth texture mostly, with a few bumpy ridges, and then he slipped it into his pocket.

"There's a small town you can go to, I think the people will be rather welcoming, there's a huge cave that'll probably have filled from the tide for you to hole up in." Vinnie recited the location of the village in which he and his friends rid the bogeymen. The town he could only think of as 'buttsweep' thanks Cooper. Anahita nodded.

"Thank you." She replied.

"Thank you, Anahita, stay safe." Waving goodbye, they made their way out of the water and watched as Anahita elegantly dived under the water and through a red spinning underwater portal.

Anahita eloquently dived, like a graceful dolphin, in and out of small puddles throughout the other realms, trying to find her way back, occasionally lifting herself up into the open to look ahead, to see exactly where her puddle leaping was taking her, and then continuing to dive through one body of water to the next. Once back in Crypskie, she returned to the hide out her friends were in, appearing in a sink full of a shimmering liquid, she lifted her head above the water.

"Anahita, you're back, we thought you'd gotten lost, or worse." Stan greeted her.

"I was lost for a moment," She sighed, then smiled. "But I found them, Amadeus and Kalmin, they're with Vinnie and some others, they're going to call when they need us, and I'll be able to open a portal close to them, we've got to help, helping them helps us, they have told me where to go, where to take some of us to be safe."

"Of course, ready everyone at your end, I'll organise everyone here, we'll be prepped for when they call and equipped to go immediately!"

Vinnie took the shell from his pocket, then replaced it back into his pocket a number of times after inspecting the little contraption every time, it did not change, it did not have buttons, it did not look magical or gave off any kind of fairylike force, he concluded that for the moment as far as he could tell, it was just a shell. The entrance to the pyramid was a huge archway covered in gold and intricate little designs, hieroglyphics that none of the friends could read, but they were so detailed and cleverly carved into the stone with what must have been an artist's steady hand. Stepping through the arch it became very dim, with just the slightest glints of gold every so often. Brushing his hand against the wall, Vinnie continued to lead the way, he touched something solid on the wall and produced a lighter from his pocket, pointing toward the object he smiled and lit the small wall sconce. Wonderfully, it lit the way and the friends watched as the fire jumped from sconce to sconce, lighting the path ahead of them and bouncing off the glittering golden specks on the walls and floors, creating an almost golden disco effect.

"Excellent." Vinnie winked.

"Interesting, how, may I ask, did you know it would do that?" Eiddwen questioned.

"Lucky guess," He shrugged. "My dad used to tell me about the tombs he visited with grandad, they had these everywhere, there was always a little puzzle to figure out to get to the next bit, I know this isn't totally real, it's Intention little game, but I thought it might have some of the same aspects." Eiddwen nodded along.

"I don't know man, something doesn't feel right, I can smell something funky, and by that, I mean, like, dead, and the aura of this place, its, it's all wrong!" Cooper shivered. Vinnie raised an eyebrow.

"The aura," He laughed. "Have I met her?"

"I'm serious."

"No, he's right, I'm sensing something too," Lydia was third in line as they walked along the fire-stricken path, passing concrete walls covered in complex hieroglyphics. "Something's here." Vinnie widened his eyes at her.

"Really, you know whenever you say something like that, shit tends to go down, maybe if you keep your mouth shut, it won't." He narrowed his eyes. Before Lydia could respond with probable abuse, Vinnie stepped on a concrete slab that pressed in like a button, they heard the click and Vinnie was pushed down by Cooper as an arrow shot from one side of the hall to the other, he felt the whoosh of the arrow as it passed the top of this head. "Bollocks!" The friends ducked, weaved and dived as the walls began firing arrows at them like something out of Indiana Jones, and as they headed for an open space, they could see a wall at the end beginning to close. Racing as fast as they could whilst trying not to become sheesh kebabs, they reached the closing wall and ducked under it, the last to roll underneath was Amadeus as the wall hit the floor.

"Well, no going back now." Cooper nervous chuckled.

"I told you so." Vinnie pointed a finger at Lydia.

"Excuse me?" She sighed.

"You have to say something along the lines of, Oh I have a bad sense, or somethings here," He made his voice high pitched as if to mock Lydia. "And then it bloody well happens, every, god damn time!"

"Shut up Vinnie, if I didn't say it it'd happen anyway!" "How do you know, you could just be bad luck!"

"Don't make me curse you!" Lacey pointed her crystal at Vinnie in defence of her sister, Vinnie fake laughed.

"Curse, go ahead, make my freaking year even better, I'm only trying to save the world, why not add a fucking curse to that too!"

"Uh guys." Cooper whispered.

"Don't tempt me Vinnie!" Lacey snarled. Lydia stood in between her sister and her friend.

"Please let's not fight, we're all the good guys here." She pleaded. Eiddwen, Kalmin and Amadeus just stared at them unsure where to look or what to do. Vinnie and Lacey were often at each other's throats, even though they were supposed to be on the same side. Personalities clashing, their parents used to say.

"Guys." Cooper said again.

"Good guy, that's pushing it a little, a lot actually, he's an asshole!" Lacey shouted.

"I'm maybe an asshole, but I'm not a fucking witch!"

"GUYS!" Cooper yelled. They all turned to look at him. "We may have a slight problem."

"WHAT?" Lacey and Vinnie shouted together. They turned to look where he was pointing and were immediately confronted by fully opened tombs with animated skeletons staring back at them. And not your regular funny bones cutesy skeletons, but ugly, old, rotting, disfigured bony things that had extremely pissed off, mean and angry, expressions emanating from their bony features, probably from being woken up from their 'forever' slumber.

"Shit." It was almost like slow motion as the skeleton people climbed out of their sarcophagi and began their rampage toward them. Vinnie and the others readied their weapons and ran at the creatures, why hang around for the inevitable? Kalmin spread his magnificent wings, and flew at the first few, smashing them to the ground into pieces like dust. Amadeus climbed a broken column and used his bow to take some down from a Ledge he perched on, and Lydia and Lacey used their Crystals to fight and shatter the bones of the few that descended upon them, helping each other this way and that way with the fight. Cooper concluded that Husky form was perfect for taking apart some bonified creatures, being dog-boy he ripped the femurs from one skele-man and the funny bone from another, chomping as he did so. Eiddwen used her curvature blade to smash into one of the skele-peoples skulls, it only angered the beast and it grabbed her by the throat, squeezing with its long, cold, thin fingers, she grabbed its wrists and snapped them clean off, using its own hands to batter it in the face, she kicked the creatures legs from under it and once on the ground she stamped through its face, her foot covered in the dusty remnants of crushed bone. Vinnie rounded a sarcophagus, meeting two skeleton people at the other side. They ran at him and he clashed his blade with the funny looking spears that they carried. They were long, made from a mixture of gold and wood, with a sharp point at one end, perfect for perforating human flesh. They made a strange ding noise as they hit his blade. Dunking under one spear he smashed the pelvis of one creature that shattered into specks and as the thing fell to the ground it ended up in even more fragmental bits, the second stabbed at him with the spiked weapon, but

Vinnie swerved to the left, the spear barely missing his shoulder, and as the creature pulled back for the next attack, Vinnie was landing tall on his feet and pursued to punch the skeleton in the face a number of times, until it's head snapped back and eventually the skull rolled off of its neck bones and onto the floor, the creatures face still screeched in anger, it looked more pissed than before too, well, who would be happy to lose their head? The body continued to try and fight Vinnie, headless, but he quickly kicked the legs from under it and the frame smashed into smithereens once it hit the ground. The head growled angrily, but Vinnie caved it in with the spear its physique once held. Looking around, he realised that the fight was now over, the catacomb they were in was now filled with open tombs, many broken bones, and dust, lots of dust, throat rusting dust.

"Well, that was fun." Eiddwen coughed. She smiled. "I've not been in a group fight for a long time."

"Group fight, you used to work with others?" Lydia asked her. They met in the middle of the room. It appeared that there was nowhere else to go, four walls, many columns, a few artefacts and lots of tombs, nothing else, no doors, not entrances, no exits, not even any holes to crawl through and feel claustrophobic in. "Yes, like you guys there was a group of us, some of them were killed in the fight, but there are a few of us left," She let out a sad sigh. "But we split because we have different paths we need to take, I need to stop the beast, the twins Petra and Percy were turned into Vampires, they're on a mission to kill the alpha that turned them so they can become human again, or so the tale goes, for all they know they'll just become the next alphas, Dante was another Oringorgon with wizard like abilities, he just disappeared after his wife was killed, I'm not even sure if he's still alive, but I always hope, and then there's Vicky, a shapeshifter like you Cooper, her little sister was taken and she's gone off looking for her."

"So why didn't you all just stick together, you know, help each other, that's what friends are for, right?" Vinnie asked. He, Amadeus and Kalmin were inspecting the walls, walking along each, pushing and shoving, trying to find some kind of secret passageway, or worse, a booby trap. Eiddwen twirled her blade around in her hands.

"Friends are all well and good until you have different prospects, plus, we're all very stubborn people I guess, set in our ways." She replied. "And our missions are way more important."

"Reminds me of someone." Lacey rolled her eyes in Vinnies direction, who for once, ignored her sly dig.

She was not wrong, Vinnie was a stubborn man, but he would hate to separate from the very people that keep him going. "Nothing's more important than friends Eiddwen, the fate of the world rests in our hands and yet we will always put each other first, because we can't succeed without each other, we need everyone, even the stragglers we pick up along the way." Lydia smiled at them all, and Eiddwen smiled back.

"I know, but I'm the only real human amongst them, so I wonder if it's more human nature than the animal derivatives they come from."

"Ah ha." Vinnie said. He held his ear against a cold concrete wall, listening intently for anything that may be on the other side. "I can feel air coming from this wall." The other all joined him along the wall and pressed their faces against it. They too could feel a cool breeze.

"This is so cool, we're like adventurers, tomb raiders, there has to be a secret passage here, right?" Cooper wondered. The others smiled briefly, typical Cooper, still finding fun in the impending doom.

"That's my guess." Vinnie felt along the wall and found three little holes in a triangle shape, almost like finger holes you might find on a bowling ball. He placed his thumb, index and middle fingers in the holes and felt the inside push in slightly, then out popped a circular handle, he took a deep breath, twist it and it could reveal a doorway, also twist it and it could lead to certain ruin, weighing his options, he twisted. Letting go, he quickly took a step back as the wall suddenly began to make a mechanical sounding noise, it started to twist and turn, slide and shift in all directions until it had completely realigned. The wall was still there, completely intact but there was now an image of a man on the wall. He was huge, with broad shoulders and muscles galore, he wore robes draped in gold and wore a funny looking square hat also a shimmering golden shade, he carried a spear, not unlike those skeletons had before, but it was double ended with a picture of a star, a half moon and a sword on the handle.

"Well, that helped." Lacey shrugged. Before Vinnie could retaliate, the mechanical noise sounded again, the room began to shake, they felt their bodies vibrating, and it was as if there were an earthquake, but then a door opened up, a trap door, beneath their feet. Like a scene from scooby doo the friends fell one by one down the hole and onto a slope, slipping down like a slide. They slid for what felt like miles, it went on and on, and up and over, they bumped into each other, they rolled over each other, they screamed, even laughed, the speed and the hilarity of seeing friends slipping and sliding was great fun, but it crossed all of their minds that they may face a pit of deadly spikes at the bottom, or scorpions or flesh eating scarabs, or everything could be perfectly fine, but when does that ever happen?

16.

"We're gonna die. We're gonna die, we're going to die in a big steaming pile of painful shit!" Cooper screeched. He had gone from giggle-mode, to petrified in an instant, the slide was going on for far too long and he anticipated something deadly at the bottom.

"No, I promise you we're not!" Lydia said, each word sounding robotic as if she was sat on a washing machine. She scrambled for her crystal and held it out in front of them as they continued slithering into whatever abyss awaited them. "Prohibere." The crystal flashed blue but they continued going. "Prohibere, stabit, morabor, prohibere!" The flashes did nothing. Ahead of them the slippery slide widened and appeared to break off into separate tunnels, several tunnels, and each individual person went through a different one. They were separated, and very quickly, without warning, their sliding experience came to an end. Kalmin, Amadeus, Vinnie and Cooper ended up flying out of their tunnels and piled on top of each other in a heap, they scrambled off one another, soon realising that the ladies were not with them, they were in an empty room, with glinting torches.

The beast with the putrid rotten human bones, unpleasant, barely there cloth, eyes of an uncharacteristically pure white, smelling of vile decomposing skin, in other words, the mummy, left Lydia where she was tied and approached another figure a few feet away, it was her own flesh and blood, Lacey, and not far from her, Eiddwen. The beast had all the women held captive, but where were the others? She spotted the table in the middle of the room, and the instruments of torture laid out beside it, the tools that would be used to sacrifice the three women, so the mummy could use their skins like coats and he could gain the power of 'being human' again.

"Lacey." She whispered. "Lacey." Lacey was unresponsive at that moment, Lydia could see the gentle rise and fall of her chest, she was alive, at least. Lydia watched the mummy as it walked between the two women, deciding which one, Lydia thought. Lacey started to stir as the beast then approached her. She screamed when she opened her eyes and faced that ugly mug, the mummy roared in her face, the odour must have been fetid. She turned her head away, holding her breath and trying not to gag, as the mummy sniffed at her hair, changing its mind, it left her and approached Eiddwen, similar thing happened. "Lacey, what do we do?" Lydia whispered louder. Lacey looked over at her.

"Hope Vinnie and the others are still alive," She said, frightened. "I'm really not that optimistic on their saviour skills, but hopefully they'll surprise me." Lydia rolled her eyes.

"One day, you and Vinnie will get along."

Meanwhile, Vinnie and the others were walking along another Goldie-looking corridor, carrying a torch of fire each of which they had stolen from the walls they passed, they used them to guide their way, because although it was not pitch black in the pyramid, it was shadowy and difficult to see any potential traps, chances were, they had not stumbled on the only ones there, there would likely be more. There was no way of knowing exactly how far underground they were, it was incredibly stuffy, smelly, damp and surprisingly cold too. Cooper waved his torch over the walls as he walked, looking at all the pictures and designs carved with such precision and perfection, what it must have taken to have that much patience he would never know. He stopped at a sarcophagus propped against the wall. The others walked past him, ignoring the tomb, but he felt compelled to look, he studied it closely, it was made from a grey-black stone, it mixed with some kind of ceramic, giving it a marbled effect, with the deep black and shades of grey causing different coloured patterns to appear all over the crypt, not a design as such, just a mixture of pretty decoration. It was closed tight, signifying that whomever was inside was probably still there, and hopefully not one of those skeletons that could get up and dance. Cooper felt captivated to explore, almost lured, but he stopped himself short from opening it, nothing terrific ever came from opening a coffin in a dark corridor, underground, whilst searching for missing friends. Zilch, nada, it would possibly lead to more time wasting, fighting and injury. He still thought about it though.

"Cooper!" Vinnie called from up ahead. Looking up Cooper attained that he could no longer see them, he was deserted. Quickening his pace, he travelled in the direction of Vinnies holler.

"Vin, Kalmin, Amadeus, where are you?" He appealed. There was no answer. It was silent for mere seconds, before he could hear a scraping sound, he imagined that of a child drawing pictures with a stone on concrete, or someone reaching the end of their meal on a plate, their knife and fork scratching the ceramic as they scrape up the last bits, or, Cooper thought, could it be a tomb opening? Cooper shuddered at the thought, just my luck his subconscious whispered, he slowly turned and looked back at the sarcophagus, pleading with his eyes that it would still be sealed shut, unfortunately, he had been quite the stickler for bad fortune, it was open and it was empty.

Vinnie had inexplicably managed to find a secret door, he had not been specifically looking for one, but had by pulling on a statue of a woman carrying a vase. He had only rested very gently on it and, like alchemy, it made a powered noise, then he and the other two were spun around, the floor beneath them turning along with the wall until they made it to the other side. They were in a new chamber, and alas, it was shrouded in what seemed to be insects. Taking a stride into the open, the bugs reacted by firing, what felt like, hot magma at them. The spray, or chemical, whatever it was, burned and stung their fragile flesh.

"Shit, fucking fiery little bastards!" The three of them panicked from the unexpected pain and in retaliation commenced stamping on the things, feeling the crunch and squelch of the bugs crushing underneath their feet. It caused the remaining bugs to shoot their assassin substance rapidly, it appeared to be their survival mechanism, a painful one at that. "What the fuck are these things?" Vinnie roared as his legs began to burn, his arms not missing out on the sore action too. He jabbed his torch at them and managed to catch a few alight, they screeched at the fire, some scurrying away in fright, so Vinnie resumed with torch wielding blows, they parted every so often but continued to spray their lava like liquid.

"They're Bombardier beetles, the explosion like spray is their defence method." Amadeus explained.

"No shit!" Vinnie stamped and torched the critters, the other two following suit. "We have to get out of here." They scanned the room whilst trying to avoid becoming human melts.

"Look, there's a door." Kalmin pointed at the other side of the room, where an obvious door, although without a handle, stood.

"Yes, let's go," Vinnie turned. "Where's Cooper?" He peered all around as he jab, jab, jabbed. "Cooper!" He could not stand and take the pain, so he pushed on with the other two and together they ran through the bugs, lighting them up along the way. Reaching the door, they used the strength of three to get it open. It eventually gave way and as they ran through it they pushed it shut behind them to leave those fiery little fuckers behind.

Cooper had no notion as to where any of his friends were, he felt alone and for the first time truly anxious and afraid, his friends were important to him, without them he felt almost helpless, and as he sauntered along the passage, he felt the hair on the back of his neck stand to attention, the hairs on his arms prickled up too, and an icy shiver ran through his body, he could sense something, he felt some kind of a presence, as if something was ensuing him, and deep within his bones he detected that whatever it was, it certainly was not friendly. He took two steps further and halted. Something was right there, right behind him, he could feel it, and it was breathing down his neck. He quickly transmuted to Husky as something close endeavoured to gnaw him, dodging the semi-surprise strike, he zipped around and doubled back until he was behind it. It was not unlike the skeleton people, only a little fleshier, as if it had died not too along ago and was only in the early-ish stages of rotting. It, was a woman, whose body was wrapped in black and gold material, its arms, legs and head had once been covered too, but they had either been unravelled or perhaps torn off, she seemed to only have half a face, the half present was not particularly unattractive, in fact, Cooper would go as far as to say she would have once been very beautiful, but the other half was skeletonesk, and was completely missing the eye, just a unfathomable, dark hole, gawked back at him. She also looked quite like she wanted to eat him. Roaring, like a lion, she attempted to grab him, but Cooper galloped between her legs and ran down the walkway. Eyeing back, he saw her jump in the air, like a leaping frog, and then she seemed to just disappear, looking ahead, and her face was in his. He stopped abruptly, gulping, and then gagging at the putrid smell, radiating from her being.

"I'm not chancing biting you, don't know what I'd catch!" He yelped as she swung at him.

Vinnie heard Cooper's yelp. It was coming through the adjacent wall. There was another statue there, this one of a cat wearing a rather fetching headdress. Together, he, Kalmin and Amadeus pushed at it, anticipating that it was another secret moving wall. It made an amusing noise and started to budge the same way the previous wall did. They stood beside it and it turned, scraping the ground, again like the aforementioned one had done, and they were back where they started in the corridor again, just in time to see Cooper thrown across the room by some ugly, mummified bitch.

Lydia and Lacey screamed at the mummy to stop. Pleaded with it, but there was no compromise with a monster. Its obnoxious being had Eiddwen strapped to the table in the centre of the cavity. She was choked and chained, tears streaming from her face as the monstrous brute carved pictures into her abdomen, arms and forehead, with a small twisted knife, like she was a piece of paper. He then advanced at Lacey. She squealed at him.

"Leave her alone, take me you hideous bastard!" Lydia hollered to no avail. The beast cut Lacey's arm and collected the pouring blood in a small chalice, he drank a small bit and smiled, a smile fouled by decay and blood. Back at the table he made a ring around Eiddwen with the blood and proceeded to drink the rest. In another language he began to chant. Lydia, to her surprise could understand.

"I sacrifice this body and soul to the gods of the underworld and over world, bring to me my strength, bring to me my flesh, and bring to me my life!" He picked up a double-ended golden spear and stabbed it through Eiddwen's chest in one fell swoop, like gutting a fish, he did not hesitate, and he did not show mercy.

"NOOOOO!" The other two screamed. Lydia felt the tears ooze from the corners of her eyes as she began to cry, and she turned her head away from the scene before her. Eiddwen choked for breath, the searing pain in her chest so vast, she could almost feel her own life draining away. The mummy released the spear and a red light shone from the blood that surrounded her, it seemed to flow into Eiddwen and then her own blood began to drain from her, rising in the air like a vortex, it then flew straight into the beasts mouth. As Eiddwen took her last breath the light stopped and the beast appeared to have a face, or rather, more flesh, and that what had previously been rotted out before, looked almost new again, he was not taking their skin as Lydia had first thought, he was taking their souls, and he was sacrificing them for a new lease of life.

17.

The Mummified woman picked Cooper up by the scruff of his neck and launched him toward his friends. They caught him like they were catching a frisbee together, and gently helped him to his feet as he returned to his human form.

"Great timing." Cooper panted.

"The fuck is that?" Vinnie questioned. The mummy stood at the end of the corridor snarling at them, she tilted her head from side to side as if making a judgement on her best course of action.

"All I can say is she isn't my mummy." Cooper replied. The others snorted at him, if ever there was a time for making jokes, facing a superhuman dead woman was not it. She jumped up and clung to the ceiling like spider-man, and began to crawl along it, her movements fast and flexible like a contortionist.

"Peachy!" The four of them dodged as she endeavoured to leap on them, her body twisting like a rubber band, but instead of hitting her targets she instead landed on all fours between them like an animal. Kalmin slashed at her with his sword, managing to remove the tops of her fingers as she reached for him, she did not cry in any pain, in fact, there was no blood oozing from the tips just a dusty residue. Growling, she dodged Amadeus's steel and Cooper's too, she pulled Amadeus by his clothes and bowled him into Kalmin and the two went down like bowling pins. Cooper stabbed her in the chest and Vinnie jabbed her in the cheek, pulling out their newly dusted blades they realised it had no effect on the rotten remains, it passed through the ugly dead bitch who appeared un-phased by the whole experience, they dipped and twirled around her like they were in the middle of a trio tango, swishing and slashing to no avail, Vinnie looked in his other hand, he was still carrying the torch, the wrap she was wearing looked highly flammable, he let a smirk cross his lips as he whooshed at her with the flickering flame, but she bowed summarily, let out a booming laugh as she threw herself against a wall and scampered horizontally along it, fast like a scurrying rat down the corridor, disappearing around a corner. "Come on, I think I've found her Achilles heel, let's follow her." Vinnie put out the torch but held it close to him, he was ready to take her out the next time they encountered her but wanted an element of surprise. They hot footed it along the passage, in the direction that she had travelled, just in time to see her crawl into a surprisingly small hole in a wall.

"Oh well, brilliant, we can certainly fit our fat asses in there." Cooper huffed sarcastically. Vinnie rolled his eyes at him.

"Maybe we can't, but you can." He smiled. Cooper let out a loud gurgle from the back of his throat.

"Of course," He sighed. The dogman could fit in there. He thought for a moment, wondering why he was cursed with such a ridiculous 'gift.' Morphing into his doggy alter ego, he sniffed around the hole and recoiled in disgust. "Uh, gross, it smells like dead rat in there."

"Nothing you're not used to then." Vinnie replied. Cooper looked back at him in distaste, his mind wandering to unpleasant thoughts involving Vinnie and a guillotine, attempting to hold his breath, he cautiously entered the hole. He was not particularly good at holding his breath, in fact it was quite impossible as his doggy self, and he found himself very quickly gasping for air, inhaling a lungful, and smell-full, of the rancid air. Gagging, he tried hard not to be sick.

"I'm putting a rotting fish in Vinnie's house when this is all over, see how he likes it." He mumbled to himself.

"Can you see anything?" Vinnie called from behind.

"Not yet," He barked back. "But the smell is ace." He coughed. Slowly going forward he could sense the end coming, the end of the hole of hellish smell, approaching the preceding light, he stopped and listened for a moment, he could not hear a thing, no sign nor new smells of life, so he exited the hole, yelped as he unexpectedly fell a couple of feet before hitting the ground on all fours, shaking himself, he took in his surroundings, it was quite a plain room, extraordinary, nothing there, nobody there, just him and another hole on another wall. "Great, alternative holes, could my day get any better." Crossing the room he abruptly stopped as the floor began to shake, he could feel his paws lifting from the ground and imminently spikes began to protrude from the ground, one by one, they popped out from underneath him, like a dog on an agility track he jumped and flipped and weaved between the spikes, yelping at the near misses. "Shit!" He stopped short of the second hole as a spike erupted in front of him, he raced around it and leapt into the hole. He was safe for a moment, he felt his heart pounding like a drummer in a rock band, his body trembled from the terror and adrenaline, he could not be totally sure he was unharmed, but in that instance he was okay. Taking in a long, deep breath and mentally telling himself to keep his shit together, he continued onwards through the second hole, his senses on full alert as he was anticipating some sort of trap to commence at any given moment. When he made it to the next room unharmed, he very guardedly entered like prey checking for predators, soon, his mind was elsewhere as he realised this one was full with gold, coins and treasure, like a pirates dream. He accosted with the utmost care and undue attention, vigilant and equipped to retort, light on his paws, he trotted to the middle of the room, where a huge mirror, sat in a grand, unique, iridescent frame, stood tall like a centre piece, surrounded by sparkly gems that twinkled like stars. He gently eased toward it, scoping the area as he went, reaching the mirror, he eyed it, doggedly, before he peered into the looking glass. At first it was just his dog, then human reflection as he regressed to his ordinary stance, then the glass shimmered and wobbled reminiscent of water, and then it revealed Vinnie, Kalmin and Amadeus. They were right where he left them, still waiting for him in the hall.

"Vin." He said. Vinnie looked up and turned to face Cooper, looking straight at him. "Can you see me?" Vinnie nodded at him then he pushed at the glass, but his hand went straight through and nearly slapped Cooper in the process. "Whoa!" Vinnie pulled his hand back and then walked straight through the mirror and stood next to Cooper. Kalmin and Amadeus followed suit. "You nearly took me out!"

"Sadly not." Vinnie shrugged. Cooper scowled.

"How'd you know to walk through it?"

"A mirror appeared in that hall out of nowhere, I knew it must be magical," Vinnie said. "Although, I was scared for my life."

"Scared, we've faced worse than magic mirrors." Cooper replied, chuckling.

"Yeah, but it had your ugly mug in it." He laughed. Cooper's face turned to a frown.

"What's wrong with you, you're really being an asshole at the moment?"

"Nothing, I'm always an asshole."

"Well ain't that the truth, dick!"

"Let's not argue, we're all experiencing this together, it's exhausting, we're all stressing probably with the sense that we're nearing either the rest of our lives or the end of the world, it's enough to make anyone –" Kalmin stated, but Cooper interrupted.

"Get their knickers in a twist?"

"We are soon going to find our fate; I think we're all getting somewhat agitated." Amadeus said.

"Let's just find the girls," Vinnie snarled. "Do you think they'd notice if any of this treasure accidentally on purpose went missing, there's enough to not notice a little magically disappear right?"

"You have a huge inheritance from your parents Vinnie, what do you need treasure for?" Cooper studied some of the jewels that were piled eight-foot-high in front of him, the delicacy of each design and the colours of the rainbow that shone through them was absolutely astonishingly mesmerising.

"I don't know, it's cool."

"I would suspect that if we took just a single coin it might cause something to materialize, magical cause and effect, anything could happen, like more of those skeletons, or mummies." Kalmin suggested. The others nodded, they all agreed that when it came to magic, it was like playing with fire, dangerous without knowing the full potential, and in such a place, magic was ubiquitous.

"Yeah, like a ripple effect." Cooper said. With that, they heard a scream, it sounded very much like Lydia. Exploring in the direction it came from they discovered that what they thought was a huge mural on the wall, was in fact a majestic door, tall to the ceiling, swathed in rainbow jewels of variable forms and dimensions, and the door happened to be slightly ajar, convenient. Alas, to their dismay, as they approached they were stopped by a rumbling below their feet, and in front of the huge exit, rose a creature, that was glowering at them with milky eyes, it had the body of a leopard and the head of a snake, a Serpopard, a foul conniving brute that enjoyed the kill, and it sure was ready to cause chaos. Charging them, Vinnie wasted no time in pulling his gun from his pocket this time, he could hear Lacey and Lydia calling for help, so he began shooting at the formidable beast. It slithered its head from side to side, dodging the bullets swiftly, its feet pounding the ground as fast as it could. Cooper shifted and met the Serpopard halfway, bounding onto it and knocking it over. They rolled on the floor, snapping at each other, the Serpopard managing to cause a deep cut in Cooper's front leg, he yelped and scrambled away as Amadeus chopped the head off the snake, a clean cut, and it fell onto the ground with a great thud.

"The art of distraction," Cooper coughed, back in human shape he clutched his right arm that had three very clear and deep scratch marks dripping with blood. "You need to learn how to be a better shot." Vinnie shrugged.

"It's not easy shooting a snake," He picked up some golden coloured cloth from one of the piles of treasure and helped Cooper to wrap it around his arm. "Are you okay?"

"It's just a scratch, I'll be fine."

"Let's hope it wasn't poisonous."

"Most venoms are held in the saliva or teeth of these kinds of creatures, you'll probably be fine." Kalmin said. Cooper snorted.

"Thanks." They heard another scream and raced toward the door, clambering through it they stumbled upon Lydia, chained to a concrete table, blood surrounding her, and a really, fuck ugly, half humanoid, beastly mummy man stood over her.

18.

The average human would probably have taken the easier, and much less calamitous action plan, they would refrain from going in there all guns blazing like Rambo on a mission of survival, but instead, creeping in, taking the rotter down before it had even noticed their presence and saving the girls in there damsel in anguish state, they would never live that down if Vinnie and Cooper were anything to do with it, and when it comes to Vinnie and Cooper, they are the shoot first ask questions later kind of guys, and being all action packed hero types, in other words, catastrophic saviours' with occasional good fortune, they have rarely thought about their situation before acting upon the state of affairs, and it is true that there is always fire where their smoke starts. The Mummy thundered at them, terrifyingly gaunt with its odd human head and skeletal from, and said something in a unique dialect, like voodoo, they saw dust and rock rise up, moving through the air in a blizzard, and again they found themselves in battle with skeleton people, soldiers Vinnie conjectured, that is what all the spears were about. The she-mummy appeared out of nowhere then, hovering above them, clinging to the ceiling like she was covered in glue, inopportunely, she was not, she flipped down quick as a wisp, flopped in front of Vinnie and immediately attacked without thought, Vinnie was ready as they began to fist fight, throwing punches, giving and receiving a good battering, most to the face causing blood to spurt from his nose and dust to puff from hers. Kalmin, Amadeus and Cooper fought the mummified soldier skeletons, breaking bones and removing skulls practically resembling an elephants' graveyard. Lydia wriggled her arms and legs in an attempt to break free of the chains, they clinked and clanked but they were too tight, the Mummy man looked at her with his new smooth, yet eerily unnatural face, a smile prominent, he lifted his arms, a blade in one hand, the goblet in the other, and he began to speak in his Arabic tongue, Lydia shook her head with an overwhelming fear that encapsulated her body as she trembled and continued to struggle.

"Vinnie, please, I need help, now!" She shouted.

"He's going to kill her!" Lacey pulled and kicked at her restraints but was unable to budge them. Vinnie ducked away from a heavy punch the mummy bitch threw, and directed his powerful punch at her kneecap which perniciously snapped, broke off the lower part of her leg and she fell sideways onto the ground as if she was a game of Jenga. He quickly produced the sconce from his coat and his lighter from the other side and flicked the lighter to light it. It did not work.

"Shit!" He flicked and flicked at it with a tiny spark visible but then de-illuminating. The bitch got back up onto one leg and continued to fling punches, missing each blow as she became slower with her missing leg and new hopping ability. "Yes!" He hissed as the lighter finally ignited and he lit the sconce, it immediately caught a flame and he shoved it in the she-bitches open mouth. She screamed in pain as she caught alight and as the flames went from a deep orange to a pure blue she burnt into a crispy, dusty pile of ashes. Lighting up a couple of the soldiers on the way to the table, like something out of a movie scene, Vinnie rolled across the floor, jumped over living and dead bones until he reached the mummy man, the monster abruptly stopped his ritual and turned to face Vinnie. He had a very narrow face, with a pointy jaw and nose, his eyes were really close together and it appeared to have not gotten his eyebrows back. Vinnie wondered how his ugly mug even wanted to be back on the planet. The brute blew out the flame and threw Vinnie across the room in one swift motion, he had an unusual bout of strength, for a dead guy. Vinnie crashed against the wall and slumped to the ground like a ton of bricks. The beast then continued his task. Cooper ran over to Vinnie, back in human form, he took Vinnie's lighter from him. Ripping the cloth from his arm, he raced over to the mummy as nimble as his friend before him, he lit it, briefly burning his hand in the process, and shoved it through the Mummies open back. The mummy shrieked in suffering, he writhed and wriggled and roared as the infernos began to encapsulate his rotten body, the heat was searing, the intensity and strength of the small blaze was mesmerising, it was as if the flames danced like tiny little ballroom dancers until he too burned into the ground. With his passing the soldiers also caught alight spontaneously until all that was left was dust and the unpleasant smell of death.

"You took your time." Lydia sighed with relief as she rested her head on the table, relaxing her body knowing she was no longer going to be stabbed and murdered.

"We got here, didn't we?" Vinnie said as he helped to unchain her.

"Yeah, at the last minute," Lacey huffed. "Always the showman right, leaving it until the last second before defusing the bomb?" She smirked. Cooper helped her out of her shackles.

"We're alive and not mummy soul food, let's just be happy and thankful we have decent friends." Lydia said, she seemed agitated as she slowly jumped down from the table.

"Are you okay Lyds?" Cooper asked. She nodded.

"After nearly dying, I suppose, and poor Eiddwen, she didn't deserve that, her body just turned to dust after he did his, thing," She paused, the others bowed their heads in unison and solidarity, briefly mourning and acknowledging the loss of someone who could have become a great friend and ally, Lydia found Eiddwen's small purse and took out the vile of vampire blood, placing it in her own bag. "I'm just unsure whether Intention is protecting herself with all these tasks to reach her, or if she has other intents, pun intended, why would all these creatures work for her like this, unless she's in cahoots with them?"

"I considered that too," Vinnie bobbed his head. "But, even if she isn't totally on our side, she can't want the King of Beasts to rise, she's a powerful sorcerer, he'll enslave her, she won't do well with that, so I think she has as much to gain from our stopping him as we do, so for now, I think we have to have some, not much, but some, trust in her."

"Fuck me, I happen to agree with you actually," Lacey said, surprising herself and the others. "She's probably bargained with these monstrosities to keep her home from invasion, there's no saying what the King of Beasts would do with her power, so I think we're currently all on the same side."

"So where do we go from here?" Cooper questioned.

"I think I may have found it." Kalmin said from the other side of the room. He was stood in front of a huge hole with a sign above it that read.

  'You're Intentions must be true, if you've made it this far."

"We have to go in there?" Cooper gulped. He bent over slightly to investigate it, but it was pitch black, there was no way of seeing how far down it went, or what was at the bottom.

"For all we know it's a bottomless pit." Lacey shuddered. Kalmin spread his wings.

"I can fly," He laughed, everyone made the 'oh yeah' face. "I'll check it out." He jumped into the hole and tilted his wings forty-five degrees to a slow glide and kind of floated down and down and down, it was pitch black, complete and utter darkness, as if he was nowhere, just empty space.

"Kalmin," Vinnie bellowed from somewhere. "Are you okay?" But Kalmin did not answer.

"Kalmin?" Amadeus called too, looking into the pit and then at the others. "We can't just leave him."

"We won't." Vinnie replied.

"Okay genius, what do you propose we do, he flew into the pit and has disappeared into nothingness?" Lacey snorted. Vinnie sighed.

"I'll go in after him."

"You can't do that, what if he's fallen on spikes, or been eaten by some ugly pit monster with green eyes and gangly legs and giant buck teeth, you don't know what's down there?" Cooper explained. Amadeus raised his eyebrows.

"Well one of us has to."

"I agree with Vinnie and Amadeus, we have to do something," Lydia said. "He could be fine; he could be in trouble."

"Then let's go." Vinnie nodded. The five of them stood side by side. "If we don't make it, it was great knowing you guys."

"It was indeed." Lydia smiled.

"Yeah I guess, kinda." Lacey shrugged.

"At least it's one way of going out knowing we did what we could to save the world." Cooper chipped in.

"Let's go already." Amadeus jumped into the hole followed closely by the others all making their own distinct yips as they began the freefall. It was silent on the fall. No sound, no feeling, no sense of anything at all, the friends could not see each other, they could not even be sure if they were all falling at once. It was a very sudden feeling, almost unreal, that they were in fact no longer falling at all, they could hear a faint buzzing sound and were jolted through a bright light and suspended in mid-air. The five friends yelled as gravity came back to them and they ended up crashing onto the green grass below them.

Kalmin helped them up.

"Sorry I couldn't tell you where the hole went."

"No shit Sherlock, I mean not a problem." Vinnie looked around. They were in a field or meadow. Vast, mostly grass with what appeared to be sections of flowerbeds full of poppies, roses and daffodils. Not too far in the distance they could see the house they were looking for. "There it is."

"Unfortunately, we have company." Cooper pointed to the beings standing between them and the house. The friends got their weapons ready; they were not going to get this far and lose.

19.

The 'red suits', normal, average looking men you might see on a day out with wives and children with their nine to five jobs, cutesy dogs named Fifi or Fido and a house with the little white picket fence, but these guys were different. They were notorious monstrosities, and although they looked decent on the outside they would kill without hesitation. The King of beasts right hand men in battles from centuries ago, made to look, well, like average Joe's, like they would not hurt a fly, but wielding the secret strength of a hundred men that sparked like a light inside their torsos, they could rip a spine straight out of the back or an oesophagus from the throat with one hand. They were also incredibly difficult to kill, almost immortal, but their only known weakness, as far as many magical creatures knew anyway, was their fear of water and inability to swim, drowning was the only way to kill them, or at least the only one that had ever been documented as truth and tested. They were identifiable as 'red suits' purely from the red velvet suits that they wore, each had a distinctive skull broach of varying colours on the left breast pocket, otherwise they just looked like smartly dressed men to the untrained eye.

The fight ensued but the friends knew they could not win this one with weapons or wit, they needed a river or even a big puddle, fast.

Vinnie felt his throat being crushed as one of the red suits grabbed him like a rag doll and tightened his grip, the suit was continually battered on the head with a sword by Amadeus, and although the red suits head bled and became disfigured, his grip did not lessen. Kalmin flew at a couple of them, swooping and swerving, until one of his wings was grabbed and ripped clean off his back. Kalmin shrieked in distress, the pain and discomfort so excruciating that his vision became blurred, he blacked out and fell to the ground as his back poured with blood. Cooper managed to rip a nose clean off the face of one and a few lank fingers off another, but they were not phased, it was as if they felt no pain. He raced around in husky form as a distraction whilst Lydia and Lacey used their magic to remove a flowerbed and dug, digging deeper until they had a pool sized hole. Touching their crystals together and holding their hands above the hole they chanted;

"Et illis sequentibus consurgetis de terra arida in stagnum aquarum aeternitatis." They repeated the chant several times as the hole began to fill with a cool murky liquid. When it was full, Cooper rounded up, then raced away from three of the red suits who chased him, their eyes on the prize, at the last moment, Cooper jumped like a show dog over the hole and the three red suits went tumbling into the water with a distinct splash. They thrashed and kicked and yelled, until their heads dipped under the water and they were gone, their bodies floated briefly back to the surface before sinking to the bottom.

Amadeus hacked the arm from the red suit that had his hand around Vinnie's throat, it let go. Vinnie fell wheezing for sweet air and coughing up his guts. The red suit followed Amadeus as he lured him to the pool, the red suit grabbed Amadeus's hair and pulled, but Cooper pushed the two of them into the liquid. The red suit panicked and began gasping, letting go of Amadeus, the Elveen swam to the side and climbed out. The red suit drowned, and he too sank to the bottom. The friends rushed to Kalmin who was alive, but barely conscious.

"That was easier than I expected, red suits are notoriously hard to fight, usually." Vinnie snorted.

"Maybe against people who don't know what they're doing?" Cooper gulped.

"Where's the last red suit?" Lacey did a three sixty but could not see the red coated mother fucker anywhere.

"Forget about the red suit, we have to get Kalmin to Intention." Vinnie and Amadeus hoisted Kalmin onto their shoulders, carrying him to the entrance of the house. It was like something out of a horror movie, dark, tall, menacing, the kind of house you would be telling the characters not to go into. Of course they were on a very important mission that if unsuccessful could cause the fall of all humanity, so they bypassed the fact it looked like a death trap and knocked on the door using the large door knocker, it was black, scaled and metal, the face of a dragon with a ring in its mouth. The sound of the bang, bang, bang rang out into the outdoors and even though it would have ricocheted through the house, no one came to answer the door.

"She has to be home; she can't not be here!" Cooper growled. He tried the handle to no avail, then rapped at the door several more times before beginning to kick it too.

"Uh, Cooper." Lacey whispered. He could not hear from all of his banging. "Cooper, the knocker." But he had already noticed the glowing pink eyes from the dragon knocker. Before he could react, the knocker flew from the door in gusts of swirly wind and grew bigger and bigger, into, what can only be described as a rather large and fearsome dragon, jagged black scales covered its entire body, pink and purple spikes protruded along its spine to the tip of its tail, it had huge clawed feet and two giant, leathery wings that were also a very dark rosy colour. The friends stared in both awe and fear, their minds whirring as they watched this fierce creature grow, a dragon, a thing of dreams and a monster of nightmares.

"How do we kill a dragon?" Lydia shrieked. The beast roared at the top of its lungs, a sound penetrating the surrounding atmosphere for miles upon miles, sending shivers down everyone's spines, it stopped its show of brutality, and slowly bowed its head, without warning it began blowing its hot, searing, face-melting flamethrower breath at them. The friends were stunned but not enough to die by bonfire, as they were able to dive to the ground avoiding getting their eyebrows, or worse, singed off. Kalmin cried out in pain as he was thrown to the ground, Vinnie helped him back to his feet whilst Amadeus jumped up and pulled out his sword. His sword was that of an Elveen warrior; a mixture of silver and rose gold metals, giving the blade a two-tone shine, the handle was a magnificent white, with intricate golden leaves delicately wrapped around it. He was angry now, his eyes glinted with a hint of red as he approached the fire breathing dinosaur. It roared in his face and again attempted to burn him to a crisp with its fire breathing capabilities, but, Amadeus was too quick, he swiftly dodged and his sword made contact with the dragons' neck, causing a long, painful wound to erupt a dark red ooze. It whipped its tail at him and swiped with its claws, but Amadeus was quick on his feet, he ducked and dived and jived his way around the beast before stabbing it in its back legs and stomach. It stomped away from him in discomfort, making growling noises of distress and anger, but he followed, Amadeus was not about to let this thing get away, he was furious, jumping onto its back, without a second thought, he brutally plunged the sword through the dragons neck, pushing with great force through muscle and organs until it passed all the way through to the other side of its neck. It cried out, a disheartening sound, then collapsed to the ground. Amadeus jumped off and joined his friends again as they watched the body of the dragon dissolve, there were tiny white lights left where the dragon had lain, and they lifted into the air like stars before disappearing into the sky.

"That's how you kill a dragon." Cooper whispered to Lydia with a grimace.

"Wow, remind me never to get on your bad side." Vinnie said with a wide-eyed expression as he struggled to hold Kalmin up straight. Amadeus walked over to Kalmin and hooked his arm around his neck from the other side to support the other half of his weight.

"Dragons are usually peaceful creatures believe it or not, whatever had happened to that one was unnatural, it's in a better place now." He replied. They heard a creaking sound and turned to see the door to the creepy house now standing wide open.

"Don't go into the house." Cooper laughed. He was only half joking, based upon recent events he thought to himself, 'nothing good can come out of walking into a strange and possibly magical house.'

"We're going in." Amadeus said sternly.

"Oh, it was a joke, in scary movies the characters always go into the creepy house and you know the monsters are in there, but they go in anyway and, never mind." He swallowed as Amadeus gave him a look that could potentially kill. The six of them entered the house.

20.

The lobby as it might be called, was better on the inside, from the outside the house was daunting, creepy, all kinds of eerie, it gave off the haunted house vibe. Inside, it was grand, red carpets, wooden décor, a white and red rose floral wall paper, there was a huge, magnificent, wooden staircase directly in the centre as you walked into the house, matching wooden banisters, with beautiful flowery carvings, on either side, curving up the stairs as they narrowed and widened, the red carpet continuing up them into the abyss of the dark upper quadrant.

"Where do we go?" Amadeus asked.

"She has a room here, what she likes to call foribus oraculi, which basically means oracle, its where she does all her, mumbo jumbo, gypsy, sorcerer, cursing, foreseeing and spell work, I've only been there the once when she was helping me catch a griffin that was eating peoples pets, but I think, given all the priceless gadgets in there, it's probably where she spends most of her time." Vinnie explained.

"Oh yeah, the griffin, vicious bastard he was, had to be one of the most difficult things we've ever faced." Cooper nodded.

"Except the potential king of beasts rising though right?" Lacey said sarcastically. Cooper poked his tongue out at her childishly.

"So, there we must go." Amadeus nodded. They took one more, long, stride inside, before Lydia realised that they were begin watched.

"Guys," She sighed. "We have company." What, pray tell, was Intentions problem? How much protection can one sorceress need? It was aggravating the lot of them, had they not faced enough already? From the top of the stairs figures appeared. Eight of them.

There were four Cyriocephalus, or in other words, men with the heads of dogs, all were wearing black suits with blue ties, but each dog head was a different breed, Doberman, Rottweiler, Alsatian and Dalmatian, there were two Vampires present, distinct by their glowing fangs, and a couple of skulking werecats, they had already shifted into their panther like state, ready for the fight ahead. There was a loud entourage of simultaneous growls and howls before they began their ferocious decent down the red carpeted stairs. Vinnie and Amadeus gently helped Kalmin to a chair at the edge of the room, it was beside a little table that held a lamp with the bust of a naked woman and some very odd looking little trinkets, he was weak and losing blood fast, they needed to end the fight and get to Intention as quickly as humanly possible in order to save the life of their friend, he was not complaining, he was brave and probably in more pain than could be imagined, of course Vinnie had no idea what it must be like to feel your wing being ripped off of your body - he had no wings. Cooper wasted no time and had already transformed into his doggy alter ego and was mid battle with the two werecats, their sharp nails clawing at him whilst he bit back with his mighty jaws. Lydia was awkwardly fist fighting with a mutt faced brute and Lacey was narrowly avoiding a bite from a couple of blood thirsty vampires. Amadeus pulled out a device from one of his many hidden inside pockets, it was a small green orb, he squeezed it and it became a bow, complete with arrows, Vinnie gasped with fascination, so that's where he kept his weaponry, it had not occurred to Vinnie before, that he had not noticed the Elveen carrying much at any one time, alas he had his answer. He loaded it, pulled back the elastic and launched an arrow through the Alsatians head as it attempted to attack Lydia from behind, it fell with a thump, dead on the ground. He shot the Rottweiler in the leg and then chest, causing it to yelp and drop lifeless to the floor, adding a little redder colour to the already blood coloured carpet. Vinnie began his fight as his assailant launched itself at him, he and the Doberman were locked in a throw of punches, the Doberman catching him a few times in the jaw before Vinnie threw a punch to the side of the creatures head, causing it to stumble backwards, he wasted no time drawing his gun and shooting the dog faced humanoid in the temple, instant death, more blood. Cooper was pinned to the ground by a werecat and as the other skulked along as if hunting for prey, it leapt toward Cooper's head, but suddenly roared in pain as an arrow entered its body, sending it flying sideways and falling like a lead balloon in a stack on the floor. Cooper snapped at the leg of the werecat on his chest, nipping it with his pincer like teeth, the creature growled and recoiled giving Cooper the opportunity to turn on it and attack. He ripped the flesh from the throat of the werecat leaving his previous fluffy white coat splattered with ruby spatters. Dalmatian face was stabbed through the neck with Lydia's crystal after their epic fist match and as the vampires rounded on Lacey, one was shot and wounded in the shoulder by Amadeus, the other's head chopped clean off by Vinnie's blade. The living vampire roared but before it could make another move Lacey thrust her crystal through its chest and into its heart, leaving it a pile of dust. All the friends stood half up and down the stairs staring at the pile of bodies, dust and crimson sea they had been a part of creating, breathless and angry.

"How much more of this shit is there?" Cooper snarled as he morphed into his usual self. His ripped T – shirt becoming ever more shredded with each transition.

"If I know anything about Intention, it's that she doesn't do things by halves." Vinnie shrugged. As they turned to go back to Kalmin there was a man stood by him. He had dark hair and eyes, and wore an odd, rugged, brown outfit. "Who are you?" Vinnie pointed his gun at the man.

"My name is Dante," He replied, a worried look in his eyes as he held his hands up in surrender. "I mean you no harm."

"What do you want then?" Cooper growled. They slowly approached the man. He sighed, putting his hands back down by his sides.

"I can't stay long," He said. "Let's just say, without this sounding cliché, I am from the not too distant future, I'm here by magic which of course you're all pretty accustomed to, I've just come to warn you that this is the wrong path, things aren't quite as what they seem, things are going to happen and we thought we could stop it by preventing it from happening in the first place," He paused, the friends stared at him like he was some sort of mental case. "I know this sounds a little far-fetched, but you have to believe me, listen, you cannot give Inten – "He was cut off as a fist went through his back and out through his chest. He looked bewildered as he took his last breath and was pushed to the ground. The missing red suit grinned from where Dante had been stood.

"Well he lasted long." Cooper grimaced as the friends prepared to fight the unbeatable, but the red suit did not start a fight, instead, he simply somersaulted over them and legged it up the stairs, three steps at a time and disappearing along the left wing. Despite not wanting to be ripped apart by a man with the strength of hundreds, they followed him anyway. Amadeus and Lacey supporting Kalmin this time. By the time they had reached the long dark corridor, the red suit had gone. The corridor was gloomy, pathetically lit, flickering chandeliers swayed from the ceiling, hanging from the walls were badly created taxidermy, mostly ugly roadkill, consisting of crows, magpies, squirrels, badgers and the odd deer. It was unwelcoming, and the friends had a sense of danger emanating like a skulking mouse from the despair, but there was also a strange vigour-like pull, reeling them into the peril.

"I guess it's this way then." Lydia sighed, her mind tormenting her as she tried to mentally bat away the gargoyles of worry.

"Of course it is, it couldn't be a catwalk with disco lights and cheering crowds no, it has to be a scary hallway, with staring dead animals, mushy blood coloured carpet and creepy flickering lights, it wouldn't be an adventure otherwise, would it?" Cooper let out an equally big sigh. Vinnie smirked.

"Catwalk wouldn't really be fitting either, would it, Intention is a little bit odd anyway, the creepier, the better for her?"

"So, let's see what else is in store for us then." Cooper nodded, and the friends, taking sharp intakes of breath, put one foot in front of the other, and started down the hallway.

21.

It was one of those moments that felt so surreal, where one had to pinch one's self to fathom that the world you were standing in, was not in fact, a dream, but felt so much like a dream state, one that increasingly warps the imagination into a complex vortex of wonder, that it caused belief in all sorts of monstrous and wacky creatures and otherworldly surroundings, only they were not really there, or were they? Was this sense of unease, hair standing on end worry, real or just a dream? It was an odd feeling, thought the friends, like their very being was being questioned in that moment, they could not work out why it was that every last one of them suddenly felt so strange. Then, they took their first steps into the next hallway and they were suddenly floating, it was as if gravity had given up its pull and given in to the atmosphere, causing the human and friendly beasts alike to bop about in the air like balloons, weightless, feathery bags of nothingness, and some of them began to feel dizzy from the effects. The walls turned a dark shade of blue and the floor a black abyss, like a disco, purple and green lights started to flicker amongst them, like stars in the night sky.

"This, is very strange." Amadeus said, trying to keep himself upright, but the weightlessness of his body caused him to uncontrollably spin and turn.

"I feel sick." Lacey puffed out her cheeks and held her hand over her mouth, Lydia laughed as she glided above her, seemingly enjoying the bizarre predicament they had found themselves in.

"This is amazing, it's like we're flying." She grimaced as she looked over at Kalmin who was spinning aimlessly with Amadeus, blood still seeped from his torn wing, but instead of gushing to the ground, it hovered in the air like little red bubbles.

"I think this is my new favourite thing," Cooper smiled as he twisted in the air like he was one of the red arrows displaying their fantastic flying skills, then he pretended to swim in the air. "I could do this all day."

"Okay, as fun as it is to float like a flipping hot air balloon, how do we get back to solid ground and anyone see a door, where the bastard hell do we go?" Vinnie moaned angrily. He was starting to get the hang of it but controlling one's body was a difficult task when it was buoyant and airborne.

"You should know, you've been here before." Lacey rolled her eyes. Lydia scanned the area and spotted a single cluster of the star like lights, they were completely still, and the smallest flicker occurring every so often that would be missed in the blink of an eye. She air swam her way to it. Vinnie followed her.

"Is this a door?" He asked.

"I don't know." She gently touched her palm onto the lights and they immediately turned a bright white and formed the shape of a door. "I'd say yes." She grinned. The light shone so bright they both descended backwards and averted their eyes, and when the light dimmed, they watched in horror as creatures began crawling out of the door. It was like an army of ants charging their way out of their nest, crawling along the walls and floor, or what would be the walls and floor had it not become an intergalactic scene. They were grey skins, something Vinnie, Cooper and Lydia had only faced once before, their name was a nod to their appearance, they had grey skins, ugly, wrinkled, on deaths door kind of grey, they also had very wrinkled, sagging faces, grey-blue eyes, only two bottom teeth that were so large they poked out of the mouth, they were dog like in the way they walked on all fours, but they were shaped like humans, with long fingernails that could gouge someone's eyes out, although short, they were very skinny and somewhat bony, but for such monsters that looked like they were at deaths door, they would certainly rip off some limbs and shred some bodies given the opportunity.

"Shit!" Vinnie shouted. These things were easy to kill, they died like humans, but their speed was inhuman and their fingernails contained a poison that with just one prick could cause one's body to shut down, first starting with the arms, a tingling sensation, followed by a heaviness, as if the blood was being replaced by lead, until they could no longer move, then, the legs, they would burn as if set on fire until they were like melted cheese, and then the vision would deplete, leaving the victim blind before finally the heart would give in and just stop beating, then the creatures themselves would enjoy the meal, slightly liquefied human, which makes sense, considering the lack of teeth. "As long as you don't get scratched, you'll be fine."

"Great." Cooper whimpered. He counted the monsters as they clung to the walls staring back at the friends with deadly glints in their eyes. "Thirteen, unlucky thirteen, perfect."

"Well, thirteen is my lucky number actually, so this will be just peachy."

22.

Battling beasts whilst floating around like uncontainable bubbles the friends found their predicament somewhat amusing despite the obvious high chance of dying, they could not help but laugh as they clashed blades with fingernails of certain death. The grey skins fought together like soldiers in sequence, so the friends did too. Lydia and Lacey chanted with their crystals pointing together and as they uttered the word 'fulmon' blue and green bolts of lightning sprung from the ends and zapped five of the grey skins in unison, shocking their bodies with thousands of bolts until a black bloody substance began to protrude from their noses and they began to float in the air, dead. Cooper could not control the Husky version of himself in the air, so he whipped out his gun that he kept hidden in his belt and shot at one of the grey skins, the bullet shot out fast then immediately slowed down before knocking the creature on the forehead with a tiny tap. Whatever was making them float stopped guns from having any kind of impact. He retrieved his blade from his boot and as he and two of the grey skins neared each other, he stabbed one through the head, before spinning out of the way of the other one's swiping hands. Amadeus clung onto Kalmin and pulled and pushed the two of them out of the way of the oncoming creatures whilst Vinnie attacked them from behind. He stabbed one in the back and one in the head, another in the back of the neck and they all drifted off, dead as door nails. Lydia and Lacey took out another three with their crystallised lightning bolts, like thunder, booming and shocking the monsters to certain doom. That left just one grey skin left, one that was in combat with Cooper, who was a worthy adversary, but contrary to being confident in battle, he lost his concentration and unfortunately, the blade was knocked from his grasp, and as he attempted to grab it when it began to drift away, the grey skin slashed him across his chest with its mighty nails. The pain was unimaginable, it felt like he had been stabbed with a thousand daggers, it burned and stung, he could already feel the poison entering his blood stream, he would not have long to live. Vinnie, like a bat out of hell, charged through the air and booted the grey skin in the head and slashed it across the throat, it cried out as bubbling blood escaped the wound and it drifted off, weak and dying. Vinnie and Lydia grabbed Cooper, who was already beginning to feel paralysed. Air-swimming over to the light shaped door, they entered and were suddenly back on solid ground once again. Cooper collapsing as his friends held him up.

"Cooper, Cooper are you okay?" Lydia asked. She cupped his head in her hands but could see his blue eyes turning a dull yellow as the poison was taking over.

"We're not losing you Cooper!" Vinnie shouted. The others joined them, propping up Kalmin and together they walked through the only door in front of them, it was a jet black colour and had an intricate design etched into every panel. Upon entering the room, a red suit ran at them.

"Stop!" Came the sound of a posh woman's voice. The red suit obliged and retreated over to the woman who was sat in front of a table, covered in black cloth and glowing stones. She wore a floor length golden gown that that barely covered her perky breasts, it glistened in the glow of the stones on the table, upon her auburn head she also wore a golden, leafy headdress with green emeralds in a cluster in the middle and matching arm jewellery, she had very bright green eyes that seemed luminous, her outfit made them stand out and glow. The woman was Intention.

"Please, Cooper and Kalmin need your healing-"She held up her hand to immediately shut Vinnie up.

"The vial?" She asked.

"Not before they are healed!"

"I'm afraid I'm going to have to – "

"NO," Vinnie shouted. "You will get nothing unless you heal them both, now, both of them are dying." He was not going to take her usual shit when his friends were on their death beds, Cooper meant a lot to him and he could not bear to lose him like they had all lost their families. She let out a big sigh and stood. The friends lay Kalmin and Cooper on the floor next to each other. Kalmin had gone very pale from all the blood loss, and Cooper's veins were beginning to look more prominent as they were filling with the poison, they were turning black. Intention collected two of her glowing crystals from the table, approached the two dying friends and dropped them into their open mouths.

"Ad perfectam salute cura, iniurias reparare, vita vestra diebus usque ad consummationem saeculi." She chanted. Her body shone in a golden blaze, and her eyes reflected like diamonds, she held her hands above the friends, and a green smoke like essence projected from her hands and into the friends open mouths. Their mouths closed and they both began to shake and shout and arch their backs in what appeared to be great pain.

"What's happening?" Vinnie said worriedly. Intention repeated her chant and as the friends swallowed the stones and the green essence disappeared, their injuries began to repair. Kalmins wing reattached itself and all the feathers settled back into their rightful positions. Cooper's black veins began to disappear, and his yellow eyes once again became their true blue. They both took in deep breaths.

"You'll feel a little faint I suspect, but you'll be fine." Intention told them. Vinnie and the others helped them to their feet.

"Thanks." Kalmin and Cooper said together, both wobbly on their feet, but alive and kicking. Intention held out her hand with the expectation of their deal being honoured. Lydia took both vials from her messenger bag and handed them to Vinnie. He held them with one hand up in the air.

"Why exactly do you need these venoms, anyway?" He questioned. Intention took them delicately into her hands and smiled, it was not a very pretty smile, more sinister than anything.

"I need it." She said. Her eyes began to glow brighter than their static emerald green. Lydia took a step back.

"The key Intention, where is it?" She questioned. Intention laughed.

"The deal, the vial or vials as Eiddwen sadly lost her life, for the keys location, where is it?" Vinnie joined in. Intention snarled.

"There are no keys!" She shouted. The friends exchanged shocked and confused looks.

"What do you mean, no keys?" Vinnie asked. Intention held up the vials with her thumbs and forefingers, a menacing smile upon her lips.

"The king of beasts isn't locked in a cage, he is buried under ground, on holy ground, in a mausoleum, the blood, the skin, the fur, the venom of all of his creatures displayed upon the grave on the one night the super blood wolf moon eclipse occurs, they're very rare so it's difficult to have everything prepared on time, but this venom in particular that I asked you to get Vinnie, of a creature that's also pretty rare these days, is the last major ingredient we need to bring back the king." It took a moment for everything to sink in.

"You utter bitch," Vinnie roared. "All of this, everything we went through and you're on his side, what the fuck, we aren't going to let it happen!" Intention laughed again.

"Aww Vinnie and friends, good people, good soldiers, completely naïve little sheep."

"I'll kill you!" Cooper and Amadeus held Vinnie back before he attempted to slit her throat, although they felt for a moment, that perhaps they should allow him.

"No, you won't." She grinned.

"But, you're a really powerful sorcerer, you could do or be anything you want, the king of beasts will enslave you, you can't want that?" Lydia asked.

"Maybe it turns her on." Lacey rolled her eyes.

"No, I will be his queen."

"Good fucking luck with that!" Vinnie pushed his friends off of him and retrieved his gun from his pocket and held it up to Intention's head. She smiled again.

"Regis ad speculcrum." She said.

Suddenly the whole room began to spin. The friends were knocked off of their feet and began to see lots of streaking multi-coloured lights before they landed in a heap on brown, dying grass. They were in a graveyard; Intention had teleported them there. As they slowly stood up, they spotted her and a variation of beasts, big and small, of all shapes, sizes and textures, surrounding a mausoleum of grey concrete, it was rectangular in shape, with a pointed roof, like a little house, but it was covered in steel bars and on the concrete were hundreds of engravings of creatures and monstrous language. There was also a huge top hat made of stone on the very top of the roof. Vinnie jumped up, without any thoughts other than to stop the beast from rising, and raced toward Intention who turned to him quick as a whistle, smiled and with a swift flick of her wrist, the six friends were thrown back miles from the action. Standing again, the friends watched in horror as creatures, again of varying monstrosities, began to climb up and out of the ground, landing out of the skies and coming from out of the trees, hundreds of them, and all facing the friends.

"Shit." Cooper grimaced.

"The super blood wolf moon is happening in a few minutes Vinnie," Lydia whispered. "And not only can they break out the king of beasts, it makes all of his creatures stronger for the whole sixty-three minutes or however long it lasts, how will we fight all of these and stop him from rising?" Vinnie shook his head. They were doomed either way, he thought, they may as well die trying to save the world than die trying to run. He reached into his pocket for his blade and his fingers skimmed something else. Pulling it out, he sighed.

"Let's hope this works." He said as he blew on the shell given to him by Anahita.

23.

Anahita, Stan, and the other creatures alike, who remained in Crypskie after hiding the children and the vulnerable in Buthesweep, heard the deep bellowing horn of the shell being blown as it rang out through the sky, the floors, the walls, they were already somewhat battle ready, and as quickly as possible they whipped on whatever armour was available, leaving enough for each other to at least have some protection, and they chose their deadly weapons, which consisted of bows, swords, blades, spears, war hammers, daggers, katanas, battle axes, chakrams, catapults, shields and more, they were prepared for a war, each picking what they deemed their most skilful asset. As unattractive swirling chocolate brown portals opened up all over the place, when the crowds of 'good-guys' were ready and able, they began to pass through them, they entered the other side, appearing beside Vinnie, Cooper, Lydia and friends, who were all equally amazed and delighted at the sheer amount of help that had come to their aid, there were so many more survivors than what they had seen previously and so many more than they had envisioned. Anahita and her mer-people entered through a puddle portal and their scaled fish tails magically turned to human legs in a sparkling display of dazzling smoke.

"Wow, I wasn't expecting all of you, thank you." Vinnie said. Anahita nodded. Donatella and Stan greeted Amadeus and Kalmin.

"We're more than happy to help, our worlds are being taken, we're all in this together, we have to stop this, and we have to fight!" Anahita explained.

"So, let's stop the biggest beast of them all setting foot on this earth." Vinnie said, and they turned to the army of monsters, waiting to attack. The creatures had been patient, relaxed almost, just waiting for the red moon to begin, as the world slowly began to bask in an ominous bloody glow, they charged at the friends and the friends charged back, weapons in the air, bellows, roars, cries, the sounds of a beginning and end as the battle commenced. Intention started to sing, beginning the ritual as she spread more of the blood, venom and other bodily fluids and pieces around the mausoleum, as she did so, it all began to glow a crimson red, her spell had started working with the moon. Lydia and Lacey used their new zapping trick to take out Zombies, Vampires, Vampidnas and werecats, whilst Cooper was clawing and biting at a pack of werewolves, he was incredibly strong and agile in husky form, werewolves were not a difficult foe. Amadeus and Donatella were sword fighting with snake-men and shapeshifting jaguar human hybrids. Stan and Kalmin were fighting creatures not unlike themselves with axes and hammers, causing more damage than they were taking. Anahita was a great fighter, instantaneous and elegant, whilst causing mass destruction with her shell handled katana. She screeched like a banshee as two of her friends were murdered by a grey skin and a wolvenbeast. She brutally took the pair out without a second thought. It was almost poetic, the slashing, crashing, bashing, the flow of crimson red, the cries of the dying and the silence of the dead. Vinnie realised that he was running out of time. He had to stop Intention. He watched his friends fight like warriors and had the firm belief that they would be fine. He made the decision to get to Intention and take her out. Running through a group of Vampires, he took some heads off with his blade and shot down some zombies that tried to bite him.

"Vinnie!" He heard the voices of Cooper and Lydia behind him, but he was on a mission and continued on, battling his way through creatures. They tried to closely follow behind him, but the monsters were coming from every direction and killing them was slowing them down. Vinnie used his last two bullets to shoot a couple of cyclops in their skulls, hitting one dead in its single eye, they dropped like flies and he threw the gun to the ground, carrying his 'praesidium' blade in his strong hand he stabbed a couple of the mouthless Astomi in the head and chest, drove it through a wolvenbeasts jaw and sliced the throat of an ogre, causing blood to spurt from the wound like a fountain, it gargled as it drowned in its own blood. The sky was turning evermore red with each minute that passed, the whole battle ground was a sea of red night sky and rivers of battle blood. The cries of the injured and dying were loud but the sounds of weapons clashing were louder, it left a ringing in the ears that temporarily stopped Vinnie in his tracks as he turned to look at the scene before him. It was like something out of Hollywood movie, surreal to see, but knowing that his friends and acquaintances were losing their lives out there he had to stop the king. Taking out some flying, blood sucking Mananang-gals, Vinnie was just a few feet from Intention, who was still chanting and singing her spine tingling ritual. The mausoleums roof had flown off now and the air around it was spinning like a twister, where they had placed all of the bits of his creatures were no longer visible, but instead there was a circle surrounding the building that was glowing a neon red, it was cold, frosty and the grass and trees close to the crumbling structure were quickly turning to dust. As Vinnie raced toward Intention, he had only one thing on his mind, KILL. He stepped up behind her and gripping his blade tightly, he rammed it through her back, but he felt no flesh, no blood, and no difficulty pushing the blade through any cavities, instead he felt a searing pain in his back, and as he looked down he could see a Sica, a curved dagger, coming out of his stomach.

"I'm always going to be a step ahead of you Vinnie." Intention whispered in his ear. She had used a teleportation and doppelganger spell to trick Vinnie into believing she was there, in fact, the Intention that he had tried to stab was just an illusion that disappeared as the blade went in, the real one was there, but he could not see her until she revealed herself by driving her Sica into has back and out through his stomach. Kicking him off of her weapon, she smiled. "You'd have been to late anyway." He fell to the ground, clutching his stomach, the pain was not as awful as he had anticipated, but perhaps that was just the adrenaline running through his body at that moment in time.

"Vinnie!" Cooper skidded to a stop beside his injured friend.

"No!" Lydia used her crystal to zap Intention's Sica from her hand as the Gyporer attempted to use it against Cooper. It flew up into the air and lost itself amongst the fighters. "Stop what you're doing Intention, you bitch!" Intention laughed.

"I have," She said. "My work here is done." The sound of a building crumbling and crashing to the ground, caused the battle grounds to temporarily halt. As the rubble disappeared, the ground beneath it rumbled and shook and began to vanish in a flurry of mud and blood revealing a large black hole. From the hole, bones began to shake before flying together and creating an almost human shaped puzzle. Once all the pieces had fused together, it revealed a huge skeletal being, larger than a human, but humanoid shaped. It had a very large wingspan, with wings that bore no feathers, just bone, it had claw like feet and human like hands with long, sharp talons at the end. Its head was huge with twisted brown stained horns on either side, not unlike a bull, or the devil. It had no skin, no eyes, and no organs at all, but it was a menacing sight, and its frightening presence could be felt through everybody. It bent down into the hole from whence it came and retrieved two items from its grave. A black top hat with a dead red rose attached, it placed it on its head between the horns, and a staff, like a walking stick, but it was made of skin and bone, and had a distinctively bulky red ruby on the top of it. Rising from the grave the creature roared, and the rumble resonated through every being present, the bad guys cheered, the good guys trembled, for he, was the king of beasts.

24.

Lydia used her crystal to try and zap the mighty beast, but without hesitation he held up his hand, causing the bolt to disperse in the air, and using just the power of his mind, he lifted Lydia into the air and dragged her toward him. Clamping his cold, bony fingers around her neck, she could feel the strength of his grip as he began to squeeze. She panicked as she clawed at his solid clutch.

"This is your end of days." He hissed. His voice was low and sent shivers through her body. Although the agony of the adrenaline waring off and the stomach wound producing an excruciating pain and a soaking of blood, Vinnie clambered to his feet with the help of Cooper and without warning, he ran full throttle at the king of beasts, using his blade, he jarred the blade with the bastards bony arm, causing it to snap off, sending both Vinnie and Lydia crashing to the ground. The hand was still clamped around Lydia's neck, Cooper helped her to remove it in Husky form and raced away to stop the beast from taking it back, the beast roared at the top of his voice, he was weakened from having been trapped for so long, despite his probable victory, he lifted his staff in the air with his remaining arm, the ruby shone bright like a disco ball, there was a bright blood red flash, and he, Intention and all his present creatures vanished into the night. The super blood wolf moon subsequently ended, and the sky became its star splattered black once again. Lydia and Cooper raced to the injured Vinnie, who was bleeding out on the ground.

"Shit Lyds, what do we do?" Cooper freaked. Lydia struggled to heal Vinnie with her crystal, Lacey joined them and together they endeavoured the power of two, to no avail.

"He needs medical attention." Anahita, her scaled legs, and human torso dashed in blood, joined them, concern etched into her features.

"No, No." Vinnie tried to sit but grimaced at the pain.

"You need a hospital Vinnie, Intention's blade was probably made to cause utmost pain, no magic will touch it, and you genuinely need surgery or something." Kalmin explained. The friends agreed. Vinnie let out a huge aggrieved sigh, he wanted to get after the king of beasts whilst the monstrous bastard was still weak, but he knew he was in no condition to fight an imp, let alone an incredibly powerful immortal. He tried to stand again, but suddenly felt dizzy, feeble, and as he blacked out, his friends caught him.

When Vinnie opened his eyes, he was groggy and disorientated, but he soon realised that he was lying in a hospital bed. He felt the excruciating, sharp tenderness emanating from his abdominal region and quickly realised he had some sort of surgery, things were stitched together, and he was fuzzy from sedation. He could hear the usual sounds one might recognise within a hospital, but somehow things seemed ramped up, like the patients were hurt beyond comprehension, and the staff were over run with too many serious cases. He could also hear a television on beside his bed and when he turned, agonisingly to see, he saw Cooper and Lydia sat on uncomfortable chairs, watching the news. The news anchor, a handsome man with dark hair, a short beard and very white teeth, was stern, to the point in his mannerisms, but you could see the fear behind his eyes, as he explained the world was in turmoil. Things, creatures, monsters, whatever the human race wanted to call them, were coming out of the shadows and attacking, they were destroying everything and everyone within their reach and they were not showing signs of stopping, they were killing, and the world was at war. He advised those that were listening to him that it was not a hoax, that this was a life or death situation and they must run, hide, reinforce their homes by any means, and grab anything and everything as a form of weapon for protection were they to be confronted by anything remotely inhuman. He ended the news report with 'Stay safe, don't let anybody in, survive, the authorities are doing what they can to stop this nightmarish hell.' The report finished and then restarted from the beginning, with images of such creatures and the attacks that had been caught on camera, it was on a loop, they had obviously stopped broadcasting live, the world was starting to go to shit already.

"We have to get out there guys and help." Vinnie said, his voice hoarse. Cooper and Lydia turned to him with fake smiles on their faces.

"Vinnie, you're awake, thank goodness, how are you feeling?" Lydia asked, genuine concern plastered on her face.

"I'm sore," He coughed. Sitting up in his bed slightly, he grimaced as the stitches twitched under the bandages. "We have to get out there, many innocents will die, are dying, we can't sit in a bloody hospital."

"Vinnie, you're really hurt, you're not going to be fighting anything." Cooper explained.

"I can." He lifted himself up and gritted his teeth as the pain shot through his stomach. He lay back down again.

"No, you can't, you need to rest." Cooper frowned. "But we can." He looked to Lydia who nodded.

"Lacey and the others are already out there, we're going to meet them soon, we wanted to check you're okay first, the monsters are attacking, killing some, but those that can, are turning humans, for a bigger army I suspect, you're right we have to get out there and help, but you Vinnie, can't just yet, I hate to be the bearer of bad news, but you're too injured, you'll get yourself killed, and probably us too when we're trying to save your ass." Vinnie sighed. They were right of course, even he was unsure how he could be of help as dreadful in condition as he felt.

"Fine, but as soon as I can, I'm out of here and helping."

"Of course." Cooper and Lydia agreed, surprised by his cooperation.

"And what of the King of beasts?" Vinnie questioned, distain in his voice.

"The King of beasts will select humans he wants, pure and good, for their souls and hearts, he takes in the souls and eats the hearts and regains his own flesh and organs, each time he does it he becomes more powerful, he's not untouchable, we can possibly take him down, but I think we have to do it fast, so Lacey and I are going to focus on finding him whilst everyone else does their part in taking down the rest of the monsters and protecting survivors." Lydia told him. Vinnie groaned.

"Okay, then get to it."

"Are you sure?" Cooper questioned.

"Yes, keep your phones close, I will find you in a day or two."

"Okay."

"Good luck guys, and don't get killed."

"We'll try not to." Cooper nodded. Lydia gave Vinnie one last hug before his two best friends walked out of his cubicle. He scowled and gnashed his teeth as the burning pain throbbed, as he slowly swivelled his legs over the side of the bed. He carefully put his feet on the ground and stood, gently, using the bed as a support. Shuffling over to his jacket, each step a pain in ones stomach, he silently roared as he put the jacket on. Taking a few deep breaths, he checked the jacket for his blade, it was still there, along with a gun, Cooper had obviously slipped the gun in there for his injured friend, perhaps he knew Vinnie would not sit around doing nothing, and perhaps he knew his friend very well indeed. Each step he took was agonising, and as he pulled back the curtain, he felt a little faint. He thought he was hallucinating when he saw, what looked like, ice footprints on the floor. He followed them to the bathroom and upon entering he heard his name being whispered. One of the mirrors was completely covered in ice. Approaching he investigated it, touching the cold glass he had a vision of grave. It was very distinctive, he could see monsters all around but somehow he knew they could not get to that grave. Then a voice, sweet and seductive, simply said 'come' and he knew where he had to go, he did not feel odd that the compulsion to go there took over him, he believed it was meant to be, something was luring him and it was going to be detrimental to the saving of mankind. Then he heard a loud roar and screams of help. There were monsters in the hospital.

25.

Exiting the lavatories, each and every step sending shockwaves of pain through his body, Vinnie quickly held up his gun and shot a werewolf in the middle of the forehead. It collapsed to the ground and returned to its former human state, and a black ooze protruded from the wound, the bullets were silver, Cooper was not a total loveable klutz after all. He smashed a Vampidna over the head with the butt of his gun and it fell sideways, scratching a nurse who cried out as it went down. Vinnie used his blade to end the creature. His body aching and sore, his strength depleting, he was not sure how he could carry on, but he would, even if it killed him.

"The world is ending!" The nurse shrieked. She was hurt but remained holding herself up tall, she was an old nurse who quite clearly, even in dire times, liked to maintain her professionalism, and her name tag read 'Tracey.'

"Tracey, hi, my name is Vinnie, I'm a patient, and to cut a very bloody long story short, I also get rid of the bad guys for a living, and right now, you need to evacuate the hospital." The nurse stared at him blankly, then pointed at the werewolf attempting a sneak attack on him. He ducked and spun around, gritting his teeth at the pain he was in, punched the beast in the jaw and shot it in the head to end it, he gasped from the agony, and turned to face Tracey again. "Tracey, evacuate the hospital now!" Tracey snapped to attention then. She quickly got onto the hospital communications and made an announcement that all patients and staff must evacuate immediately as they were under an imminent threat, all patients unable to get themselves out safely should wait for staff, although the raucous in the hospital had already sent many fleeing. There was a flurry and a frenzy of staff and patients then, helping each other to get out of the hospital, some wheeled out in wheelchairs, some being pushed along still in their beds, the capable helped the staff to support those that could walk, or rather hobble as they were sore or medicated, others simply legged it, it was not a very organized evacuation, but no one could blame them, no one predicted a random terror attack on a small hospital, least of all, monsters that are not supposed to exist being the ones responsible. Vinnie rushed at a Shivhantay, a woman in form, but with silver knife like finger nails and teeth, a shiny bald head, grey eyes and pointy ears. Savage creatures that enjoyed the hunt and the kill, they like to slice parts of their prey off, and into pieces whilst the prey is still alive, and squirming. She managed to escape Vinnie's plunge of the blade and slashed at his stomach with her knifey digits. He yelled in discomfort as they caused not only more wounds to his already slashed torso, but the knifed fingers also removed the bandages and reopened the recently stitched wound. He held his stomach as if all his organs were about to fall out, his hands were drenched in his own blood. The Shivhantay grinned with those silvery Gnasher's and tapped on the hospitals reception desk in an intimidating fashion, the click, click, click rang through Vinnie's ears. Vinnie felt weak, faint even, so he lifted his gun, wobbly, finding it hard to focus, then pointed it at the bald headed bitch. She darted out of the way of the shot he fired and raced toward him smacking the gun from out of his loosened grip. It clambered to the floor and skidded away from them. Vinnie held up his blade and as the monster lifted her sharp members in the air, ready to stab him in the chest, a shot rang out and the creature looked down to the new hole in her chest before collapsing on the ground like a sack of potatoes. Nurse Tracey trembled as she held up the smoking gun. Vinnie, bleary eyed and shivering, hobbled over to her and gently took the gun from her.

"Thanks." He murmured. She helped to support him.

"You need treatment," She said. "There are still ambulances outside taking people to safety, let's get to one, they'll be able to help, there's plenty of supplies in them."

"No," Vinnie shook his head defiantly. "I have to go somewhere else; I know they will help me; I need a car to get there though." He unhooked his arm from around her shoulders.

"You can't be a hero if you're dying sir."

"Trust me, I'll be okay, I have to stop what's happening, I and my friends are the only ones that can do it, I need to get somewhere, now." He stumbled back and turned to leave. Tracey fished in her pocket of her uniform and produced her car keys.

"Vinnie." She called, he turned, and she threw the keys at him which he caught in one hand. "It's an ice blue BMW M5, the number plate ends in CEY, it's personalised, and you won't miss it." Vinnie forged a smile.

"Thank you, I'll try and get it back to you in one piece."

"Don't worry about it, the world is soon to be in ruins, and if you think you can stop it, I won't stand in your way," She smiled. "Good luck." He nodded and slow jogged, holding his wounds, his skin still trickling out red, and went out of the automatic main doors.

Cooper and Lydia had succeeded in finding the others in the next town over. The town was under siege by a pack of Wolvenbeasts, a stoning of gargoyles and something the friends thought were just myths; the puppet people. A description is not needed for a puppet person, they are their name. However, puppet people, although mostly made of fabrics and stuffing, were in fact possessed by spirits that were not human by nature, so they would often be taken over by the spirits of beasts, usually the evil kind, and usually hell bent on turning others into human puppets, either by literally sewing parts of people onto different people, or fabrics or buttons or whatever materials they could get their hands on, or by repossessing a weakened human, the puppet maims the human, meaning the spirit can pass into the living body, or so the tales were told.

"How do we kill a puppet person Lydia?" Lacey zapped a gargoyle to dust with her crystal whilst Lydia stuck hers through a Wolvenbeasts temple.

"Um, well their possessed right, so exorcism?"

"Yeah because we have time for that mid battle!" Cooper ripped a limb from a puppet person, and watched the stuffing fall from the newfound hole, the hand and arm sill wiggling in his mouth as he spat it out. It crawled back to its puppet master and sewed itself back on. "Okay then, fucking ace, can reattach limbs, got it."

"Then what do you suggest?" Lacey shouted.

"We have to fall back, there's too many of them." Kalmin shouted from the air, his wings flapping and gliding as he circled the friends and foes. He shot his bow several times and killed many of the approaching Wolvenbeasts, they were not particularly hard to kill, and it was their sheer size and brute strength that was worrisome. The friends ran back, nearing a building that the locals were held up in. They were shooting their guns from the side lines in a bid to help. "Get inside, we'll barricade the doors and fight from the roof." As they were racing for the doors, Cooper heard the screams of a child. He turned his fluffy head and saw a little girl cowering beside an upturned vehicle as a gargoyle approached her. Racing over with a howl, Cooper jumped on the back of the gargoyle, returning to human form he snapped off one of the gargoyles stone wings and used it to smash the creature to pieces. Holding his hand out in a gesture to the little girl, she ignored it and jumped into his arms. He picked her up and carried her to the building. Running inside, Cooper turned to watch people slam the doors closed and barricade them all in with everything they could, tables, chairs, bookshelves, cabinets, everything and anything, the girl held tightly onto his neck as he, and the mass of people, made their way up the stairs and onto the roof.

"What's your name?" He asked her.

"Gracie." She replied.

"I'm Cooper."

"Gracie!" Came a woman's voice. A blonde-haired lady raced up to them and took the girl into her arms. "Thank you." She said to Cooper. Cooper nodded as he watched the mother and daughter embrace.

"They're climbing up the building, what do we do?" Donatella shouted as she peered over the edge, Amadeus by her side.

"We fight." Lydia replied. And as the creatures began to reach the top, those fighting for survival started their attack.

26.

Vinnie had safely made it to the vehicle, unable to help the humans being maimed and eaten, they were a great, although unfortunate, distraction as he bled out whilst opening the door and falling into the car seat. He grimaced at the shooting pain as he started the ignition and putting the car into reverse, he edged out of the parking spot, bumping into another car before whacking the car into drive. He moaned and groaned as the seat belt alarm started pinging to be plugged in, they were on the brink of destruction was there really any need for health and safety at this point? But he reluctantly put his seat belt on despite the pain it caused, anything to stop that incessant dinging. As he drove along the road he could see the ruin unfolding around him. People were badly injured or lying dead or dying in the streets, beasts were too, some creatures were on the side of the humans it appeared and were helping, which made Vinnie have a sudden feeling of hope, a belief that everyone out there had some fighting chance of survival, not all beasts were bad, Cooper, Lydia and the rest of them could all be classed as monsters, but they were the 'good guys'. He veered the car into a vampidna as it hunted a man who had clearly run out of shotgun bullets. The vampidna somersaulted over the bonnet and roof, before landing behind the vehicle. Vinnie acknowledged the old guys thumbs up and continued on his way.

The fight on the roof was in full throttle. The side of the foes were at a disadvantage as the heroes were able to encounter them before they made it to the top, many of them being pushed from the side or over the side and plummeting to certain doom. Cooper heavily protected Gracie and her mother, whilst Lydia and Lacey worked together, as their mother used to tell them 'they are better, faster, stronger and think clearly as a team', their magic works in unison, they were sisters after all, and they are that little more powerful, plus spells, particularly those neither had used before, were more likely to work. Anahita and her merpeople were brilliant fighters with their katanas and tridents, whilst Amadeus, Donatella, Kalmin and Stan used swords and bows to stop many of the creatures reaching the top, they had gone from peaceful, non-confrontational beings, to absolute ass kicking warriors. The humans on the roof, although confused by the beings they thought were only real in fairy tales, fought alongside them with whatever weapons they had picked up from their homes and surrounding areas.

"Lydia, there's too many, we're not going to get through this!" Lacey kicked a gargoyle in its stoney face and blasted it with a bolt from her crystal, it spontaneously burst into lots of clumpy lumps.

"We have to try Lacey."

"She's right Lydia," Anahita chopped the arms, legs and head of a puppet person before picking up some of the body parts and chucking them over the side before it could sow itself back together, it's torso wiggled on the floor like a fish out of water. "They just keep coming, we need to get a portal going and get the hell out of here, I need you and Lacey to make as big a puddle of water as you can, and I can make a portal out of it." Lydia and Lacey looked at each other and broke away from the fight at the same time.

"Okay, we'll do it." Lacey shouted and the two of them touched points on their crystals.

◆ ◆ ◆

Vinnie parked the newly dented car at the entrance to the cemetery he felt so compelled to go to, vowing to get it fixed for Nurse Tracey should he get out of the whole predicament alive. It was not the graveyard in which the King of Beasts had risen from, but it was just as eerie and surprisingly quiet, perhaps even uninhabited, it's better to be an optimist than a cynic right? He scoped the perimeter before setting foot through the mile high iron gates. The path was gritty, gravelly and some of it, he noticed, was blood splattered, something had happened here, but whatever it was, it was over now. He took another agonising step, still clutching his stomach, he stopped for a breath, each intake rattling his bones. It was too quiet. The 'aura' he thought, Cooper would be pleased, of the place, felt almost surreal, like he was about to step foot on the surface of the moon, he was still held by a gravitational pull, but everything felt, light, airy, like he could scream and nothing would come out, or would it? Would it just not be heard? He turned to look at the gravestones beside him. The stones were there, uniformly next to each other, each name, date of birth and death clearly visible, but underneath them, where there should be lush grass, or flowers, or whatever sentimental ornaments loved ones had left to pay their respects, were actually large holes with open, empty caskets and coffins, not a pleasant sight, when the dead should be resting.

"Excellent, super fucking peachy with a cherry on top." He groaned as he heard the typical moan of a zombie. He looked behind him to see a horde, slowly making their way toward him, some quite skeletal, others with their rotting blue under toned flesh, maggot infested rib cages and parts of the body hanging off. He also caught a glimpse of more making their ways out of their underground homes, digging their way out of their crypts like moles. Beginning a staggering run, he sustained his way down the path, clutching his bleeding, throbbing stomach with one hand and retrieving his gun with the other. He shot a few in the head as they tried their assault and they dropped like flies, stinky, rotten, putrid flies. He yelped as one stumbled close and managed to scratch him on the shoulder and arm, but they failed to grab him and chow down as he shot them to the ground too. The undead, undead chased him along the path, passing more fiends worming their way out of their graves, then he had a moment of clarity and partial relief as he spotted the grave that he was looking for. It was a huge headstone. In fact, it was more of a statue, than a headstone. It was of a woman on a stage, on her knees, gigantic wings protruding from her back, there was half a halo on her head, and she had her arms raised above her head, holding, what looked like, a scythe. He raced toward it, his guts felt like they were spilling out, he collapsed at the foot of the grave and looked toward his assailants, they were closing in. He was not sure what to do, with his bloody hands he banged on the base of the grave. Nothing happened. He shot a couple of the closer zombies in search of their favourite meal, but he knew there were just too many, he gave up hope in that moment. He knew he was going to die.

Lacey was thrown to the ground by a Wolvenbeast, trying to stop her from helping her sister from completing the spell they were casting. Cooper dived onto the back of the creature and clamped his jaws around the top of its neck, it roared and began bucking, and Cooper clung on like he was in a rodeo. Lydia helped her sister up and the two of them continued their spell, watching closely as the small puddle of water they had first created, began to fill, getting bigger and bigger.

Vinnie slammed his blood covered hand upon the grave and bellowed into the night, as if he were a wolf howling at the moon. As the wretched zombies reached him, he heard a strange noise. Suddenly, he was thrown backwards, his whole body lifting off the ground sending sharp jolts of hurt through him, and he fell, crashing on stone, before he went tumbling down concrete steps and as he landed in a heap on the black, glittered, marble floor of his new sanctuary, he watched with blurry vision as the statue he had been pounding on, closed like a door, preventing the living dead from following his footsteps, or rather epic fall. It was freezing, like he was in the arctic. He groaned as every fibre of his body ached and burned. He was slowing down, fragile, losing his vision and feeling faint as the blood loss was too great. Blinking to try and clear his bleary eyes, he made out a silhouette of something, it reached down to him. A cold, icy hand touched his chest, he wheezed, gasping for air as he lost his breath for a moment, a magnificent flash of light temporarily blinded him, but he was not afraid, if it was his time to go, he had made peace with that, he was in bad shape after all. When he opened his eyes again, he was no longer in pain. His wounds, they were gone, they were healed, like magic; he was still covered in blood and his shirt was raggedy, but he had no visible, and better yet, no excruciating lesions causing him to feel so close to deaths door. Standing, warily, he looked at the creature before him.

"You," He said, recognition crossing his features. "I know you, you saved me from drowning when I was just a kid, and I knew you were okay when you called, but why, why am I here?"

"Hello Vinnie." Said the woman's voice. "Your destiny was always to stop the king of beasts rising, you're too late for that of course, and you failed, but not too late to stop him."

"Ah, well I could've guessed that's why I'm here, I just, I don't understand why you helped me then, now, are you going to help stop him, who are you, really?"

"Yes," She stepped into the light. "But I need your help too."

27.

The room itself was large, all surfaces a jet black and glittering marble, the marble, Vinnie observed, glittered because it was covered in ice. There were three gates at the other end of the room, one read, 'Bargain basement' another said, 'So you sold your soul' and the biggest set of gates, black as night, in the very centre read 'Welcome to Hell.' They were the gates to hell, all three a different level of hell, each one a different level of torture. It sent an uncontrollable shiver through Vinnie's very core. The woman, Vinnie discerned, was not unlike the statue he'd fallen through; she was tall, skeletal, almost like a line was drawn directly down the middle of her face and torso, she had half of her body covered in a sleek, white flesh and half actual skeleton. She had two little horns in her forehead, there was no halo however, and perhaps she only wore it on special occasions. She had wings coming out of her back, one of which was blooming with beautiful black and white feathers, the other, bonified, grey and white. She, Vinnie remembered reading about her as a child, was the gatekeeper. The keeper of hell. Not the devil, but a servant of him. She would help guide souls through the right gates, sometimes choosing for them, she also had the capacity to reap souls and drag people to hell, were it needed in any given situation. She had once saved Vinnie, when he was around nine years old, he fell into a river that was infested with various underwater sea monsters. He was dragged into the water and nearly drowned until this atrocious looking woman, killed the monster and helped him back to the surface. She had saved him because even back then, she knew he would be the leader in taking down the King of Beasts.

They spoke for some time, but Vinnie still was not sure about the goings on, he was not even sure he believed in his fate to take down the beast, surly someone else would be in his place were he not around? Or had never been born? He stared at the peculiar woman, thinking.   "I understand you also want the king of beasts gone, hell will be overrun by beings not meant to die yet, I get that would be an utter shit show, even for someone as mighty as you, and the devil, but why help me specifically, anyone could take him down with your help right, what can I possibly offer you, what's the cost for your help that you suspect I will accept?" Vinnie questioned. The gatekeeper smiled.

"Of course, there will always be a deal to make dear Vinnie, it's in our nature down here." She touched his cheek and it temporarily froze before warming again. He shuddered. "I had a hell hound as my right hand man, but he is missing, he was on a mission to retrieve a few hellish escapees and well, simply hasn't returned."

"Wait, you can escape hell?"

"Not ordinarily, but times have been different of late," She gritted her teeth. Vinnie cringed as he watched a snake weave in and out of her ribs before coming out through her eye socket and wrapping itself, like a scarf, around her neck. "And both he, and the very mischievous souls are unaccounted for, so I need your help to get them back, I believe the hound to be dead."

"But, what can I do?"

"I can give you power, fire power, very few humans can have it and live, believe me I've tried, but there are exceptions, like you, it'll help in taking down the beast, as can I, and it will also help me get back the prisoners, it's a win, win, Vin." She chuckled. He swallowed.

"It seems too good to be true," He thought for a moment, watching the Gatekeeper, as she walked back towards the gates. "What do you gain, apart from the escapees, what does giving me the fire power achieve?" She stood before the 'Hell gate' and turned to face him. Clicking her fingers, a long pole with a curved blade, at either end of it, appeared in her hand. A scythe of sorts, but this one was made of ice. She twisted it in her hand like a baton.

"The king of beasts isn't good for hell, there's an order, there's certain destinies that have to be fulfilled at the right time, with his and his minions killing sprees the order of heaven and hell will be all over the place, we'll be over run and escape is more likely, possessions and poltergeists undoubtedly, and with some spirits stuck on earth, some stuck in purgatory, some stuck between life and purgatory, and that's something else entirely, it may even be too much for death and his grims to handle, that people may just simply stop dying, but they will still feel pain to their bodies, they could still be tortured, and once they're able to reach heaven or hell after that, their souls will be one hell 'ova spirit to handle, souls totally blackened are difficult to contain, even in hell, the devil is just one supernatural being, his demons, his hounds, me, we can only do so much, and we cannot stop the beast alone, we're not full entities with real bodies, you Vinnie, were always meant to face the beast, whether that was to stop his rising or in person, I think something about you means you can stop him, perhaps it was engrained in you when you born I don't know, you are correct in thinking a prophecy was never made, someone else could take your place, but that could be years from now, and to put it bluntly, he is a being not of this earth, not created here, not by the almighty god, or any big bang, he was made in another realm, another galaxy by something alien to us all, and you have to stop him, and giving you the fire power will give you the advantage, not to mention the help I need to get back the souls that have been lost, I was given one hound and he was a doofus, unintelligent, egocentric man-hound, it wouldn't surprise me at all if he's just simply chosen to not bother to search at all, but to hide away like the little puppy he is, that, or like I said, he's probably dead, I prefer the latter." Vinnie digested the information with great difficulty. On the one hand, the King of Beasts needed stopping before gaining any more of his power and although there would still be war amongst his own beasts and the people it would be more manageable, they would be weakened without their master, they would fear that they would all die and possibly go underground again, plus Vinnie would gain some awesome fire power, he was not quite sure what exactly that meant but it sounded cool, on the other hand in front of him was 'The Gatekeeper' she was a monster unto her own, tales were told of how before she gained her post, she took the souls of young women and used them to create her own army against men, again this was centuries ago and some of it was real truths, whilst some of it was lies, the story would be ever more fabricated over the years by various different story tellers, but still, could he trust this creature? After Intention's clearly evil intentions, he was not sure he could trust anybody.

"You have a good argument," He nodded. "But I don't understand why I am the only one that can stop him." She angrily ripped the snake from around her neck and squeezed it until its body popped, the sound was gut curdling. Taking a deep breath, she seemed to calm herself.

"Honestly Vinnie, some things are meant to be, you, are meant to be the one in this time, give it a century and there'll be another, only earth will probably be baron, along with the help of your particular friends, with the added boost from me, you are capable, and should you fail there will be others who will try." She walked toward him and stopped just inches from his face. "So, what'll be, you get my help, you gain a super power, you stop that beast, but you help me get back those souls, make your choice?" Vinnie frowned, did he really have a choice?

"Okay, let's do it," He agreed. "One more question." The Gatekeeper sighed. "Why is it so cold down here, its hell isn't it, shouldn't my skin be boiling, into…boils of hotness?" She laughed.

"It's true, with each level of hell you descend to it does get hotter and hotter to the point a human body would melt," She smiled. "But the gates of hell, well, they're so cold it burns."

Cooper was ripping up a puppet person like a rag doll as Lydia and Lacey had created a pool on top of the building. Anahita broke free of the fight and dived into the water. Her legs became a fin once again. Twirling the water, she began a chant in her mermaid tongue, getting louder and louder, faster and faster until a whirlpool was formed and it got bigger. It suddenly turned a purplish-blue and twinkled like a star as it spun.

"It's working," Anahita shouted above the commotion. "I can't seem to direct it anywhere though!"

"What does that mean?" Cooper yelped as his tail was bitten by a gargoyle.

"I'm not sure where exactly we'll end up." She replied.

"Oh, well, as long as we don't end up in a pit of giant, mega-horned, poisonous scorpions, then it'll have to do." Anahita managed a roll of the eyes before finishing her spell.

"It's ready." She said.

28.

"Wait, wait, another question," Vinnie said as the Gatekeeper looked increasingly frustrated, if a half human, half skeleton can look any more frustrated. "How will I, with whatever power you give me, be able to catch these escaped souls, will I just know how to do it?"

"The fire power will give you an instinct alongside your own Vinnie, but you will also work alongside me, probably a few reapers and the angel of death who, is temporarily unavailable, but, she'll be ready when the time comes."

"The angel of death," Vinnie shrugged. "As long as she doesn't, death, me." The gatekeeper sighed.

"She won't."

"Okay last question," He smiled. "My whole, fated to kill the king of beasts is a load of bull isn't it?" The gatekeeper laughed and nodded.

"You are an Oringorgon, you are strong, you have the will that I need to give you this firepower and bring back the lost souls," She explained. "But you are correct, you alone are not the messiah, the chosen one, the one to defeat evil, you are just well equipped with the potential of doing so, you can possibly defeat him, that is true, but, together, there is a chance we can send him to purgatory, limbo, and it's impossible for him to leave without someone of my stature, or the devil, maybe the odd angel and demon could release him, but none of his little minions, including that Gyporer bitch, will ever get him back out, I thought perhaps if you thought you were meant to do it, it'd get done quicker."

"I'm not that stupid, give me some credit please, that still doesn't explain why you saved me that time though, as a kid?" Vinnie said candidly. She shrugged. "I saved a lot of Oringorgons Vinnie, one of you had to be the one to stop the real shit from going down, like I said, you, now, are prepared, willing, strong and able, you would die to see that beast go down, and that's what I'm looking for in a prodigy, so to speak."

"So, let's do it then, let's send that ugly bastard to limbo, or wherever the 'not' hell he can't get out of."

"It'd be better if he was dead but there isn't a definite way we've figured how to kill him, but limbo is the plan b."

"Okay, agreed," Vinnie took a deep breath. "Fire me up then." The Gatekeeper smiled. She pulled a dagger from thin air into the palm of her hand, it was sharp, covered in a black, soot-like, substance and it had specks all over it that glowed bright orange, like lava.

"This is going to hurt," She said. "A lot." Without warning, she thrust the knife into the very centre of his chest. The pain was instantly unbearable. He could feel the blades sharp point breaking the skin and the lava heat searing his flesh. It burned into his body, he could smell his singing skin, and as he doubled over in agony, the pain, the burning and breathlessness began to overwhelm all his senses. His veins began to glow orange through his skin and his eyes shone a mixture of brown and orange. His whole body caught alight like a ball of fire and he screamed in suffering until suddenly, the fire extinguished itself. His body was smoking, but he was perfectly intact, and his eyes turned back to their natural brown again. He looked like Vinnie, he was normal him again, but he felt different. He felt powerful, he felt strong, and he felt like he could do anything.

"Thanks for the warning." He choked.

◆ ◆ ◆

"Everybody, jump into the portal!" Lydia shouted. She, Lacey and Anahita used a combined spell to hold off the bad guys whilst their friends and the people they had saved hopped into the puddle portal, immediately disappearing into an unknown abyss. And once everyone had gone through, Cooper, Lydia, Lacey and Anahita followed close behind, Anahita causing the portal to collapse as she was the last to enter.

The Gatekeeper stood at the bottom of the steps, she clicked her fingers and transformed herself into a beautiful human woman, her hair black as night, but cut like a pixie, Bright blue eyes and a tall, slender body. She wore a pair of leather trousers and matching leather crop top, showing off a stomach that was covered in demon-like tattoos. She squeezed her scythe and it shrunk to a more manageable size.

"Let's be gone." She said. They made their way up the marble steps and out of the open statue. The zombies began their slow limping toward the pair in a bid to eat them. "First lesson, look at the zombie you want to kill, raise your hand toward it, think fire, release fire, go." Following her command, he did as she asked. His hand briefly ignited and went out again. "Think, I'm going to die if I don't work this shit out." He tried again, failed again. As the zombie got closer, Vinnie took in a deep breath, he thought of his friends and how he wanted to see them again, the next thing he knew, he felt the heat and the power of his hand igniting, like a flamethrower, the fire blew at the zombie, setting it alight. "Excellent." He continued his new found flame-throwing abilities to take out more of the walking doomed until the pair made it back to his vehicle.

"Get in," He said, as they both, swiftly, jumped into the car. "So, where to?"

"Drive on Vinnie, we'll get where we need to go." Vinnie rolled his eyes, of course it would be that easy, and he put his foot down, hard, on the accelerator, ploughing through more zombified remains as he began rolling down the road to his victory, to his death, who knew at this point? Either way he was going out in style.

The portal closed behind Anahita and as she fell through the void of swirling colour, she was caught by one of her merman friends. The whole crew was there, Lydia, Cooper and the rest of them, along with the people they had saved. They had landed in another part of the country, one that was already dishevelled by monsters that had moved on. There were still some buildings intact, and some movement beyond the walls.

"Let's search for survivors," Cooper said. "I don't think the beasts will be back."

And so their journey continued, to find and help those in need, and to rid the earth of as many beasts as was possible. They worried for Vinnie, but they knew he would be safe, he was Vinnie the Oringorgon after all.

Meanwhile, the lair of the most brutal beast found deep within a jungle, in underground Aztec ruins, Intention walked a hypnotised human female down an aisle to the foot of the King of beast's throne. His minions, beasts and ghouls of all species, stood and watched as the beast lifted her into the air with his mind. He pulled her toward him and with his remaining skeletal hand, he put it over her mouth, made a guttural throat noise and pulled his hand away, taking with it a ghostly form of the woman before him, her soul. He sucked it in like a drink through a straw, then viciously punched his fist through her chest and ripped out her heart. He let the dead woman tumble to the ground in a bloody heap. Holding the heart in the air he grinned. Then he tore into it, eating it like a savage animal, and once all was consumed, he let out an ear popping roar. He looked at Intention who smiled. For there were now red eyes in the once empty sockets.

TO BE CONTINUED...

Made in the USA
Monee, IL
09 December 2020